# THE MIDDLE SCHOOL MEAN QUEENS

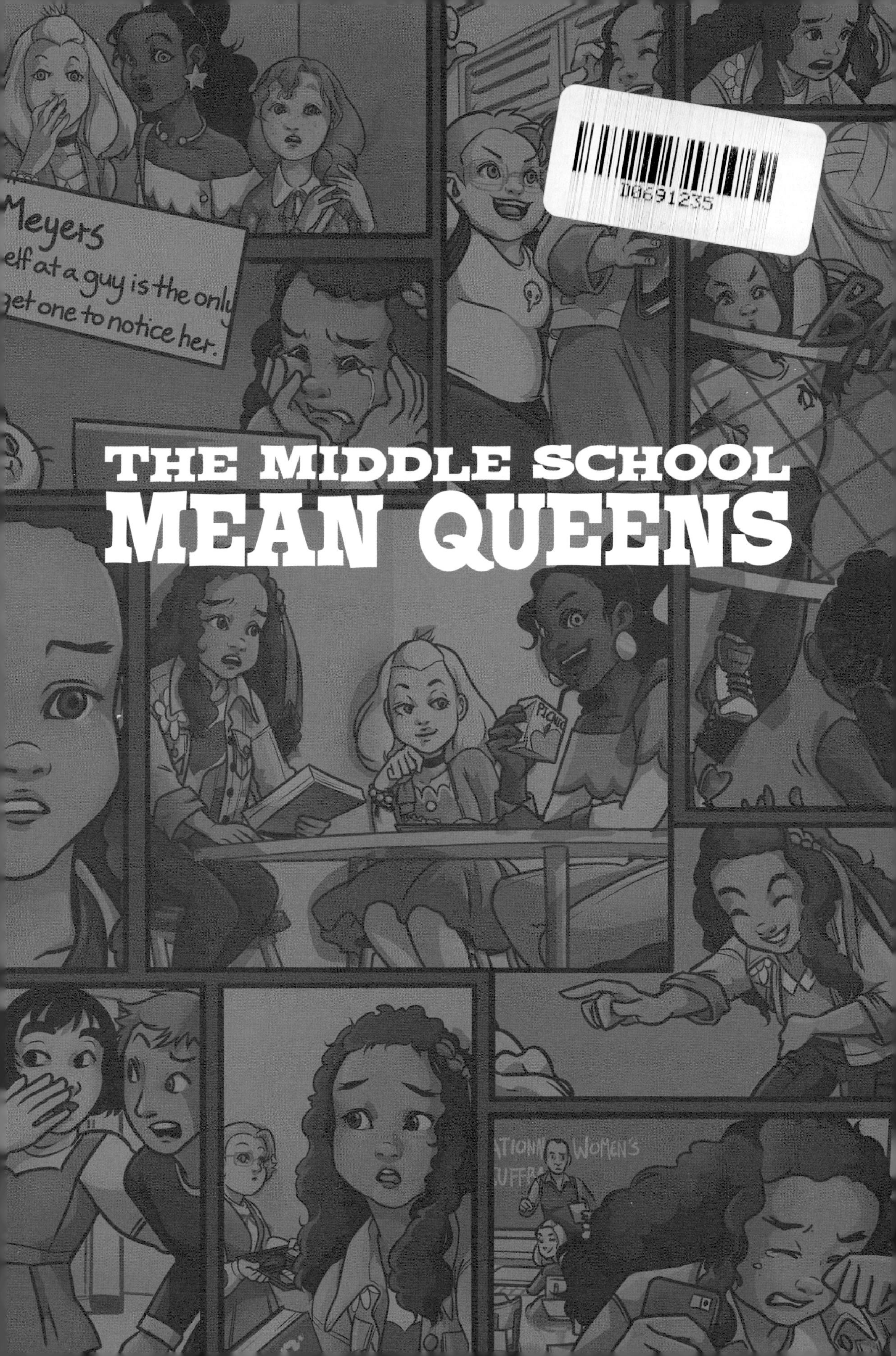
Meyers
elf at a guy is the only
get one to notice her.
PICNIC
WOMEN'S

JUNIOR HIGH DRAMA IS PUBLISHED BY
STONE ARCH BOOKS
A CAPSTONE IMPRINT
1710 ROE CREST DRIVE
NORTH MANKATO, MINNESOTA 56003
WWW.MYCAPSTONE.COM

Summary: Lilly wants to hang out with the popular girls, so when queen bee Tania invites Lilly to her birthday party, she can't wait. What she doesn't realize is that Tania is hoping to go through Lilly to get to her cute older brother, Hank. When Tania's plan fails, she blames Lilly, making her life a nightmare. Will Lilly survive the mean queens of middle school?

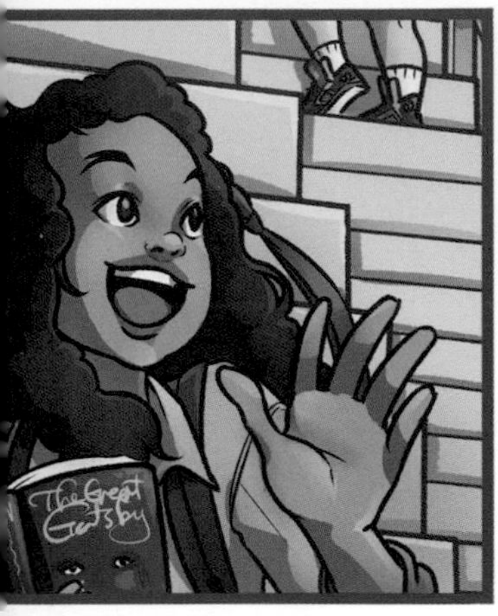
The Great Gatsby

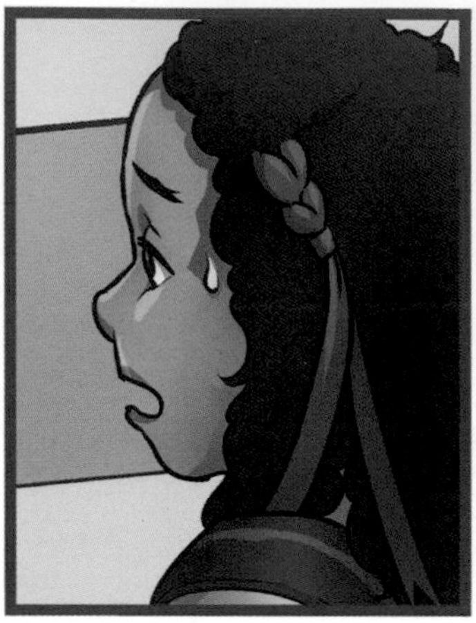

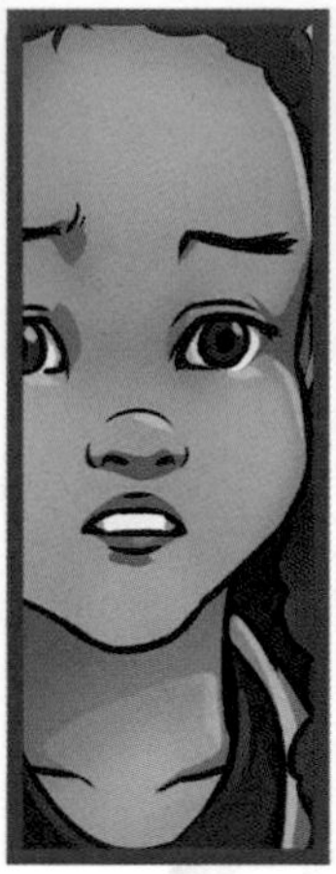

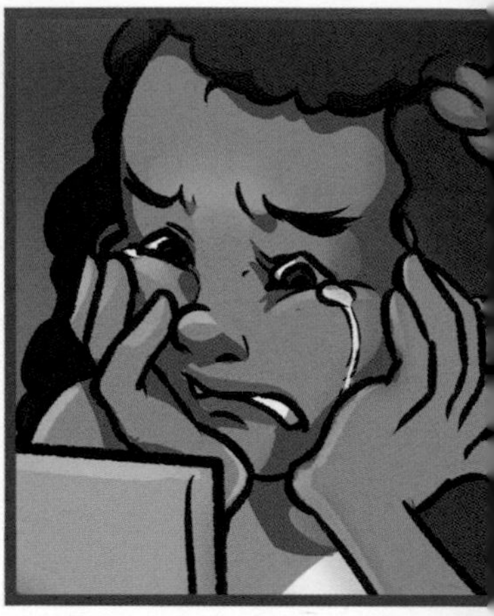



CATALOGING-IN-PUBLICATION DATA IS AVAILABLE ON THE LIBRARY OF CONGRESS WEBSITE.
ISBN: 978-1-4965-4710-1 (LIBRARY BINDING)
ISBN: 978-1-4965-7412-1 (PAPERBACK)
ISBN: 978-1-4965-4715-6 (EBOOK PDF)

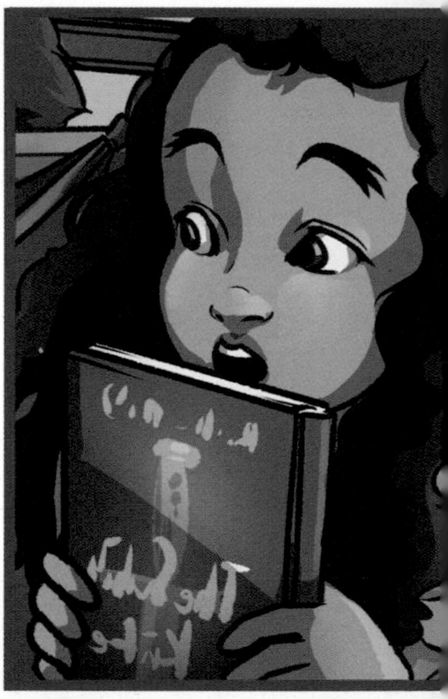

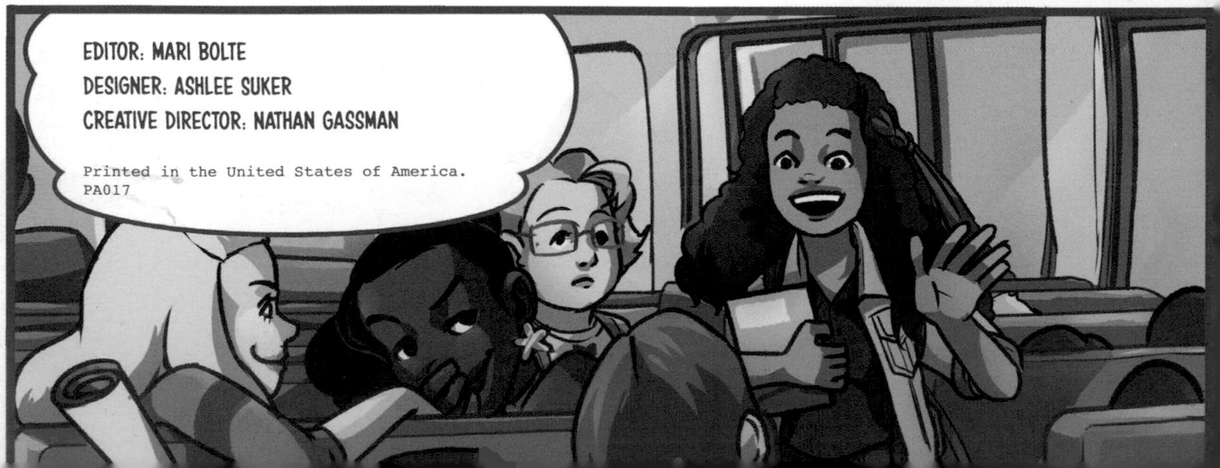
EDITOR: MARI BOLTE
DESIGNER: ASHLEE SUKER
CREATIVE DIRECTOR: NATHAN GASSMAN
Printed in the United States of America.
PA017

# JUNIOR HIGH DRAMA

# THE MIDDLE SCHOOL MEAN QUEENS

by Louise Simonson          illustrated by Sumin Cho

STONE ARCH BOOKS
a capstone imprint

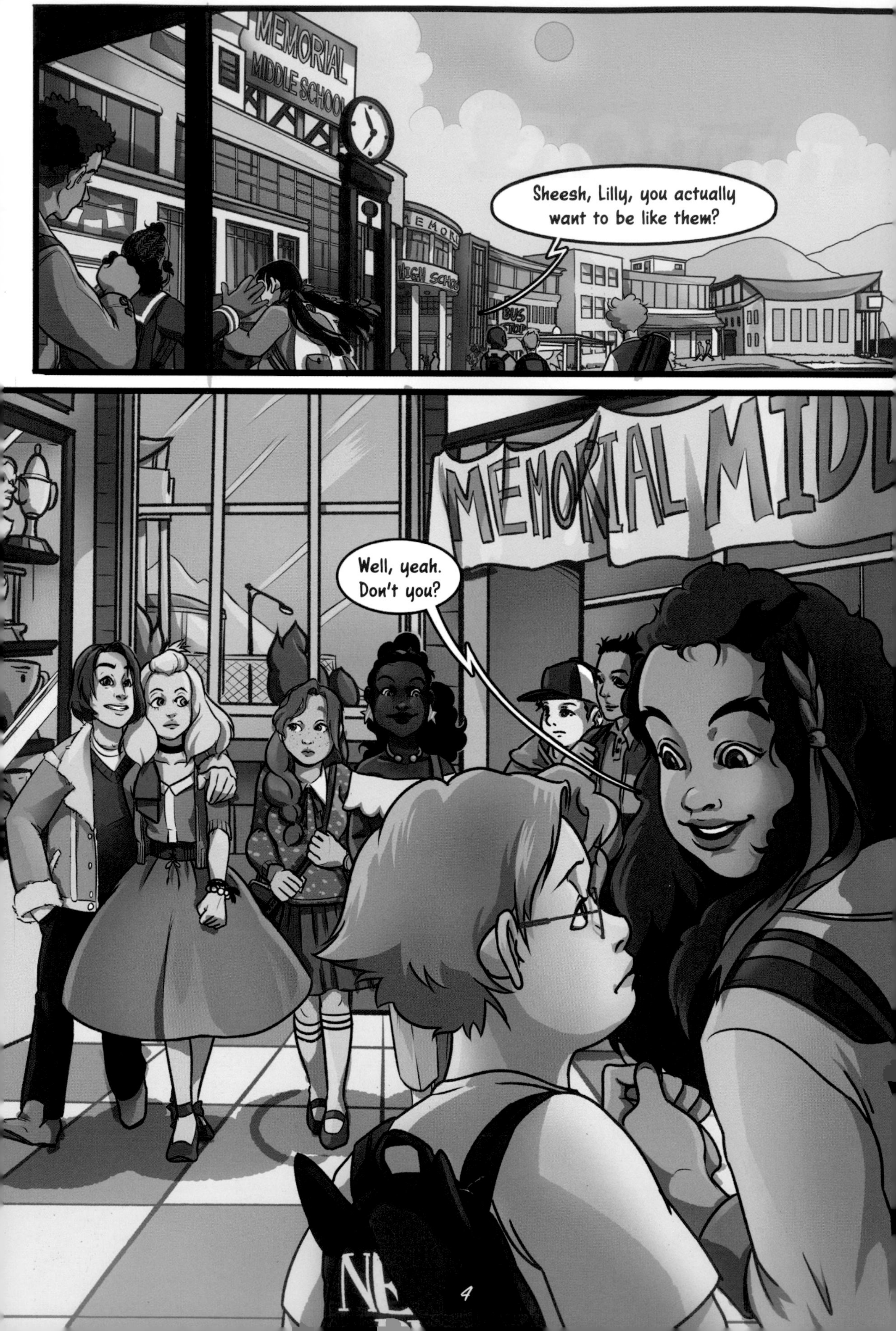
MEMORIAL MIDDLE SCHOOL
BUS STOP
Sheesh, Lilly, you actually want to be like them?
Well, yeah. Don't you?

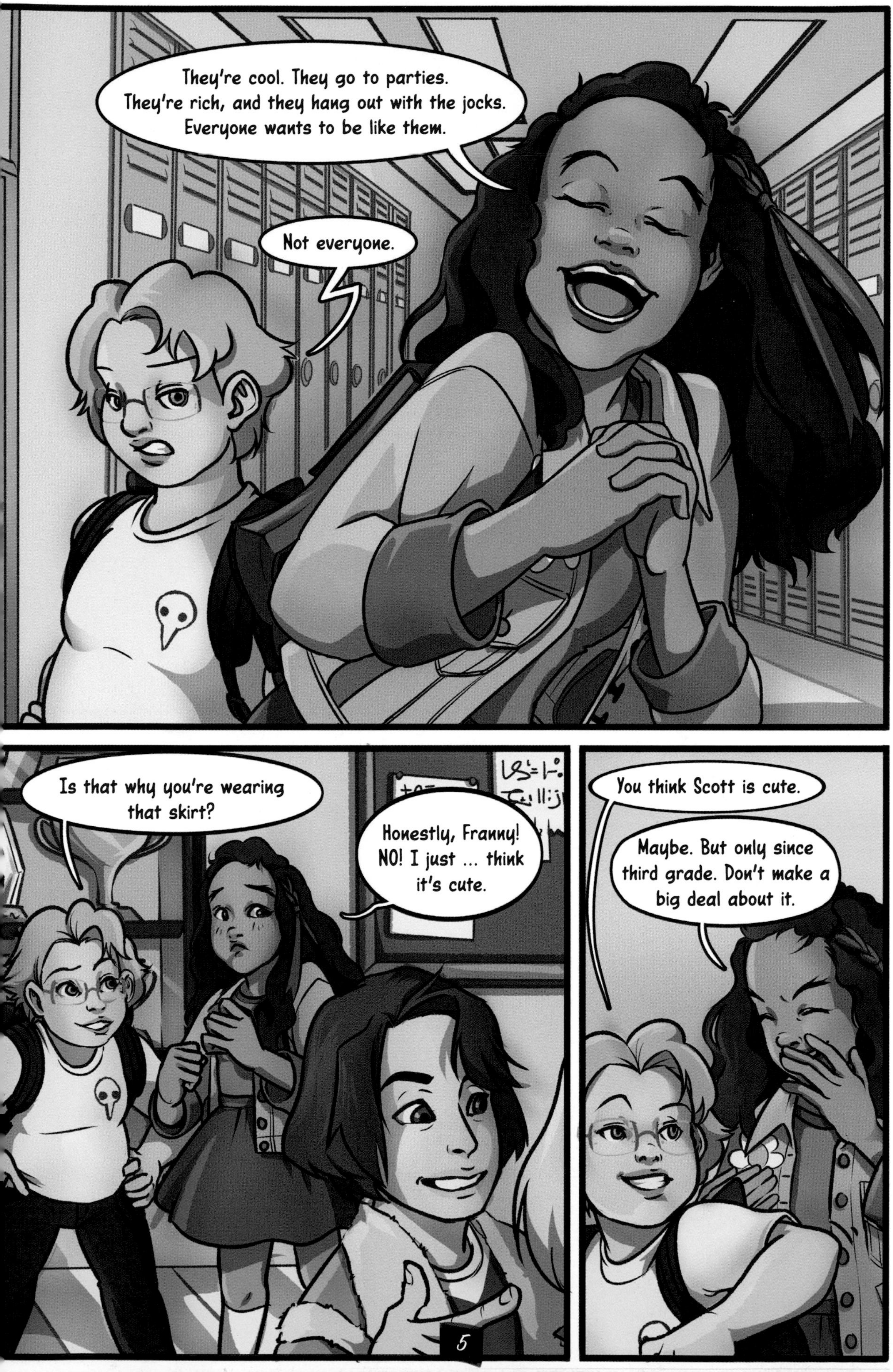
They're cool. They go to parties. They're rich, and they hang out with the jocks. Everyone wants to be like them.
Not everyone.
Is that why you're wearing that skirt?
Honestly, Franny! NO! I just ... think it's cute.
You think Scott is cute.
Maybe. But only since third grade. Don't make a big deal about it.

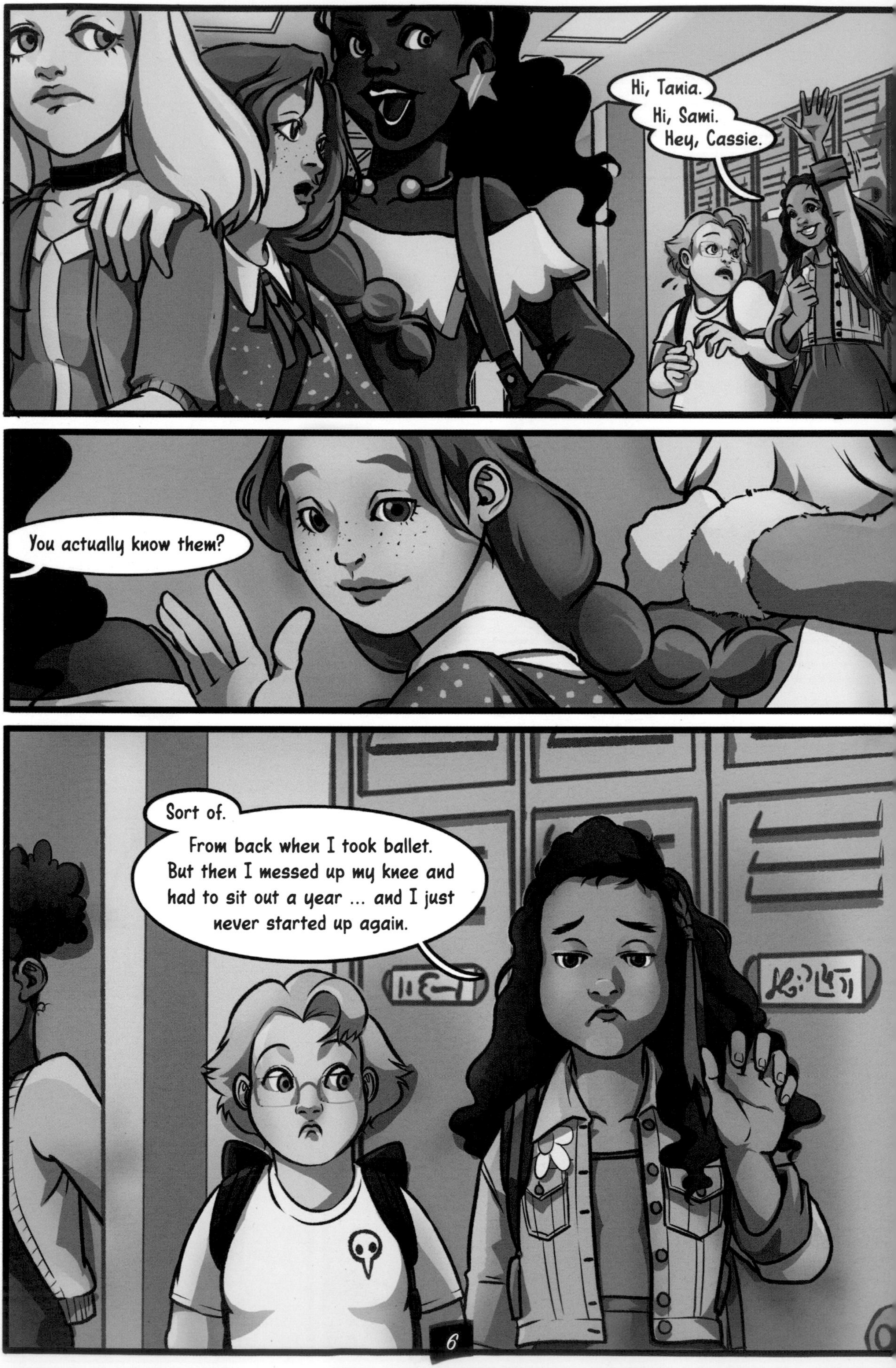
Hi, Tania.
Hi, Sami.
Hey, Cassie.
You actually know them?
Sort of.
From back when I took ballet. But then I messed up my knee and had to sit out a year ... and I just never started up again.

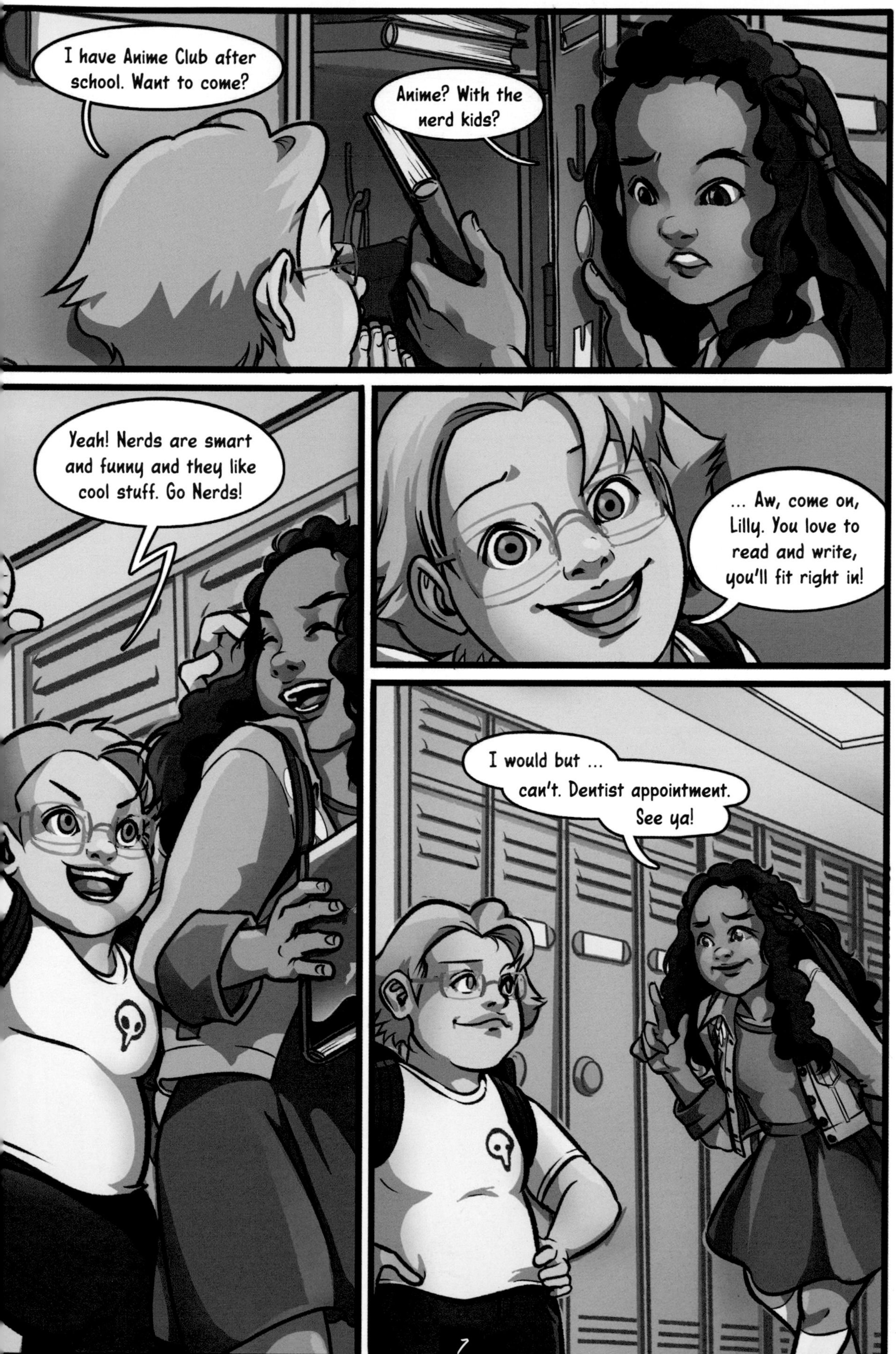
I have Anime Club after school. Want to come?
Anime? With the nerd kids?
Yeah! Nerds are smart and funny and they like cool stuff. Go Nerds!
... Aw, come on, Lilly. You love to read and write, you'll fit right in!
I would but ... can't. Dentist appointment. See ya!

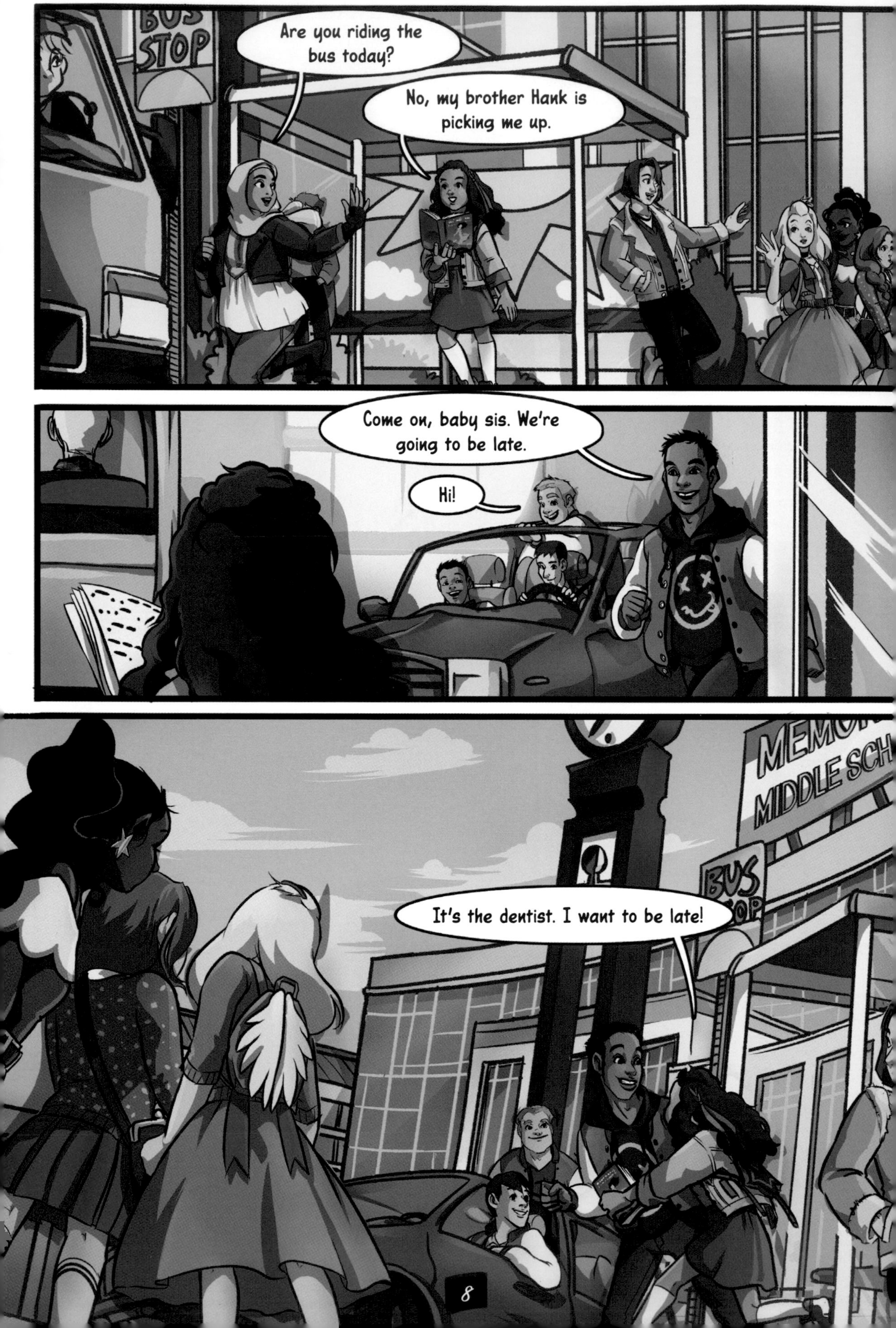

BUS STOP
Are you riding the bus today?
No, my brother Hank is picking me up.
Come on, baby sis. We're going to be late.
Hi!
MEMO
MIDDLE SCH
BUS
It's the dentist. I want to be late!

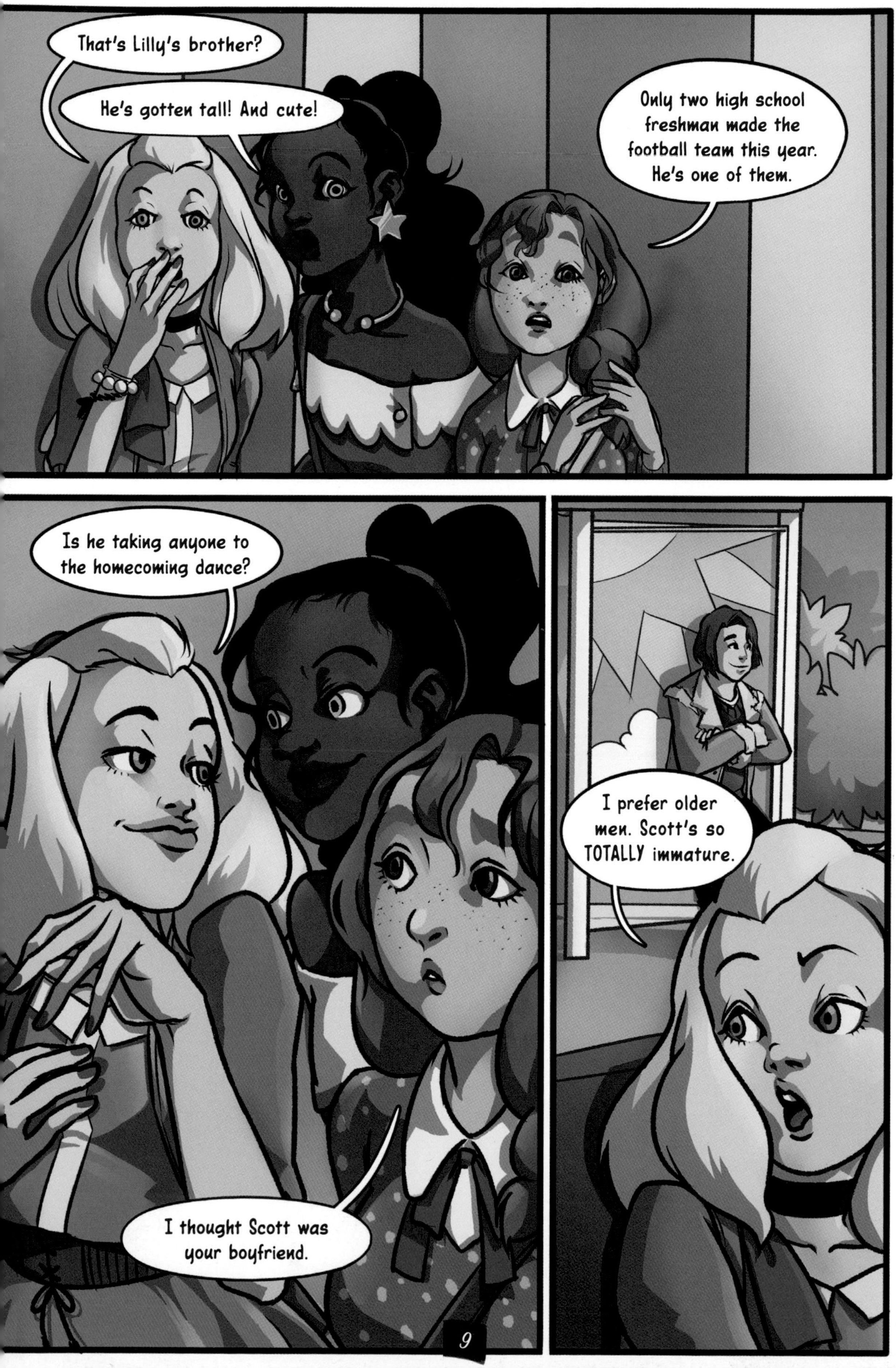
That's Lilly's brother?
He's gotten tall! And cute!
Only two high school freshman made the football team this year. He's one of them.
Is he taking anyone to the homecoming dance?
I thought Scott was your boyfriend.
I prefer older men. Scott's so TOTALLY immature.

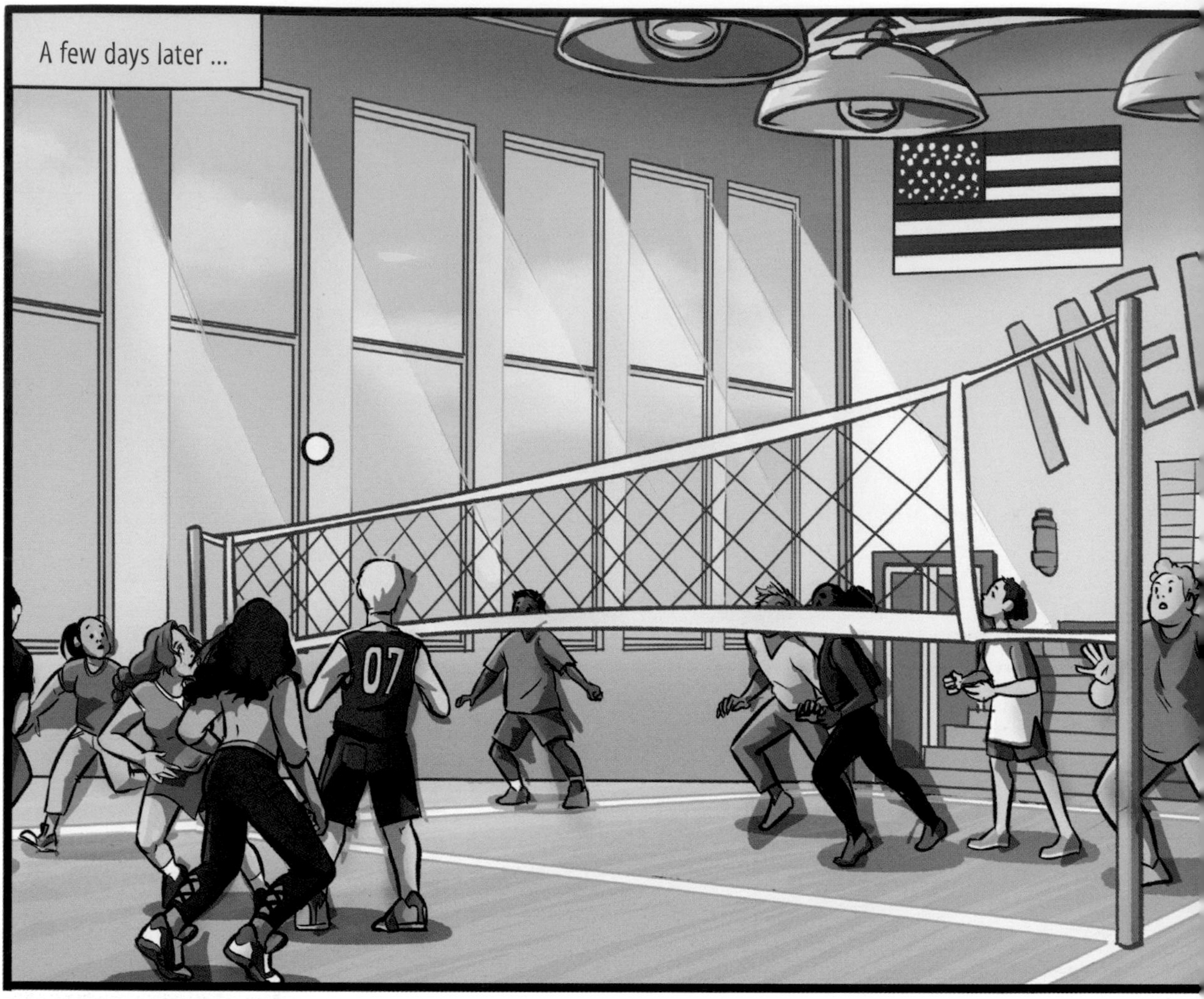
A few days later ...
07

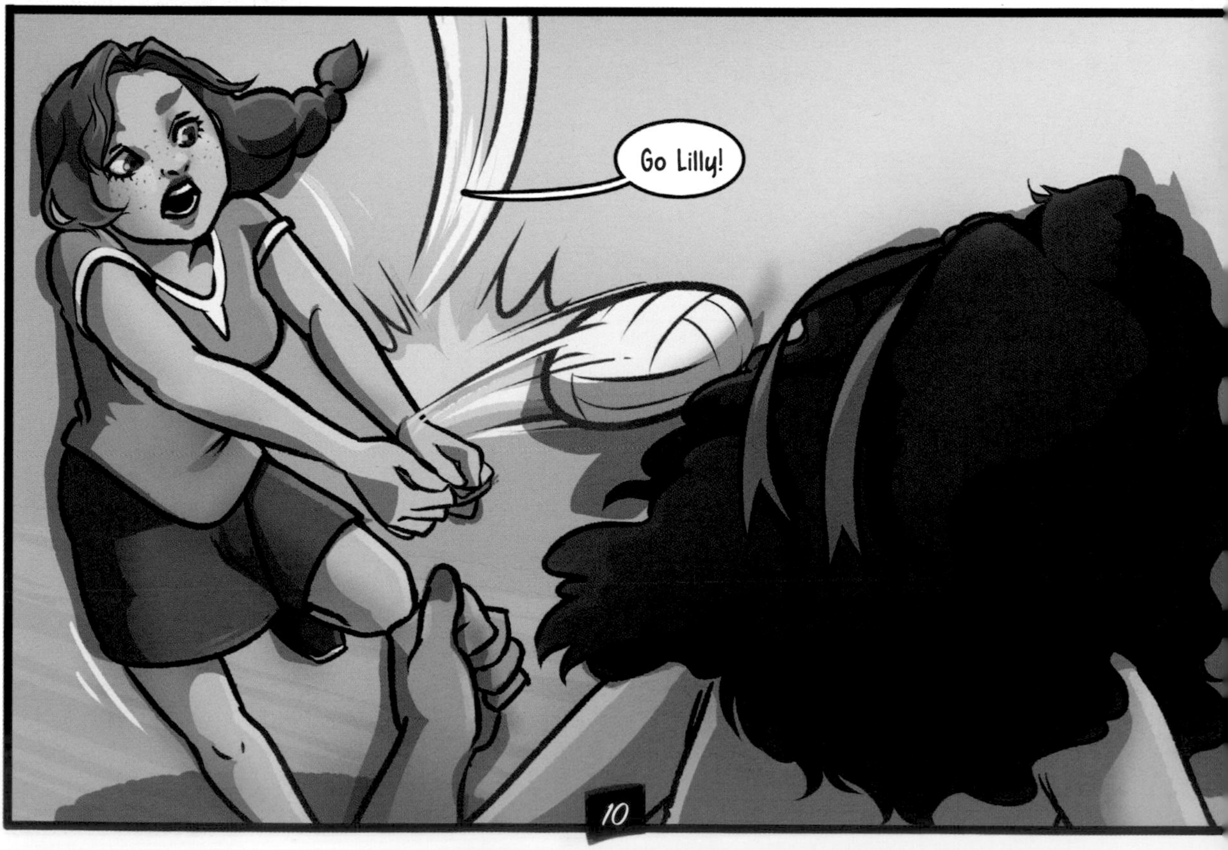
Go Lilly!

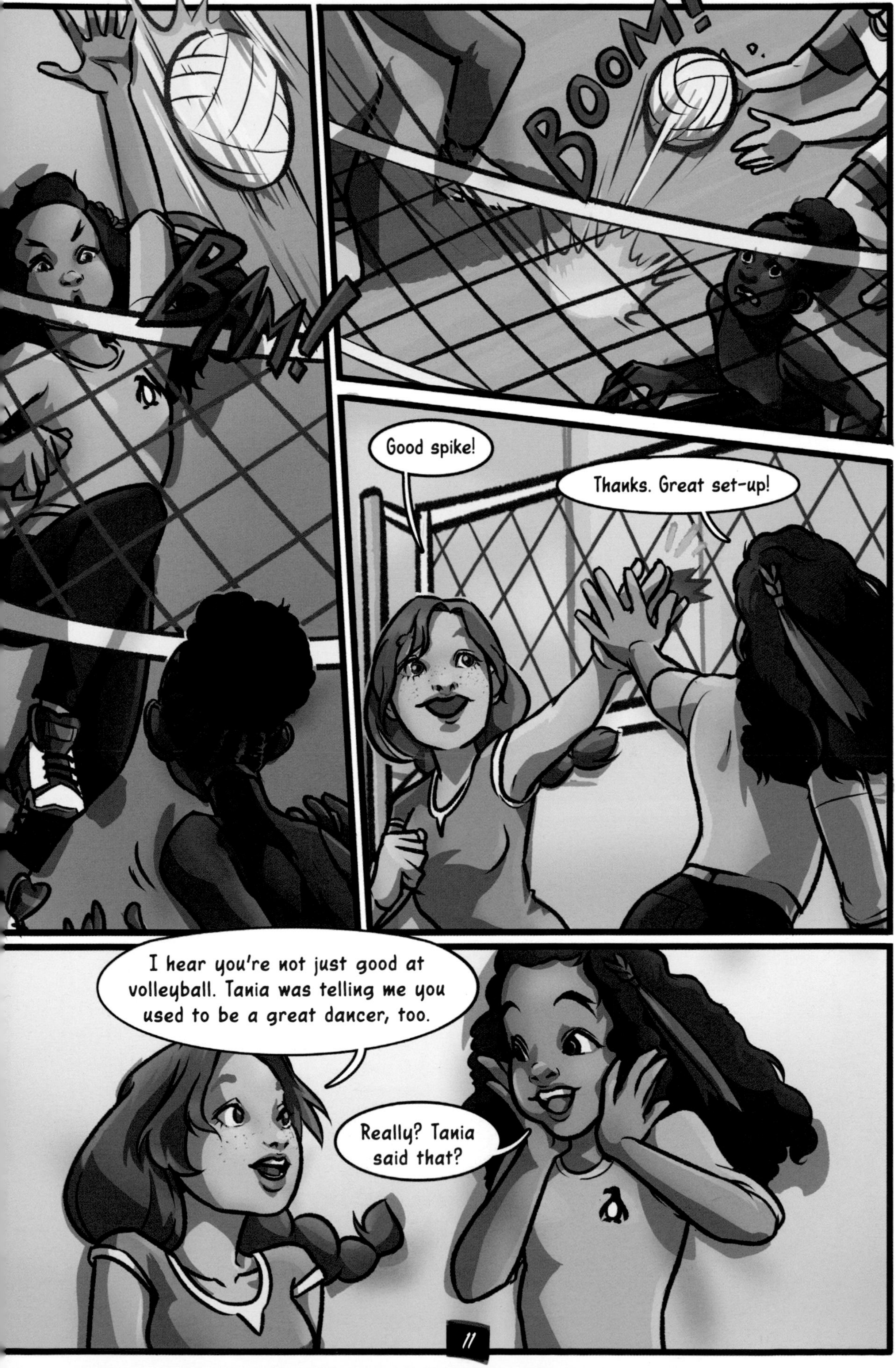
BAM!
BOOM!
Good spike!
Thanks. Great set-up!
I hear you're not just good at volleyball. Tania was telling me you used to be a great dancer, too.
Really? Tania said that?

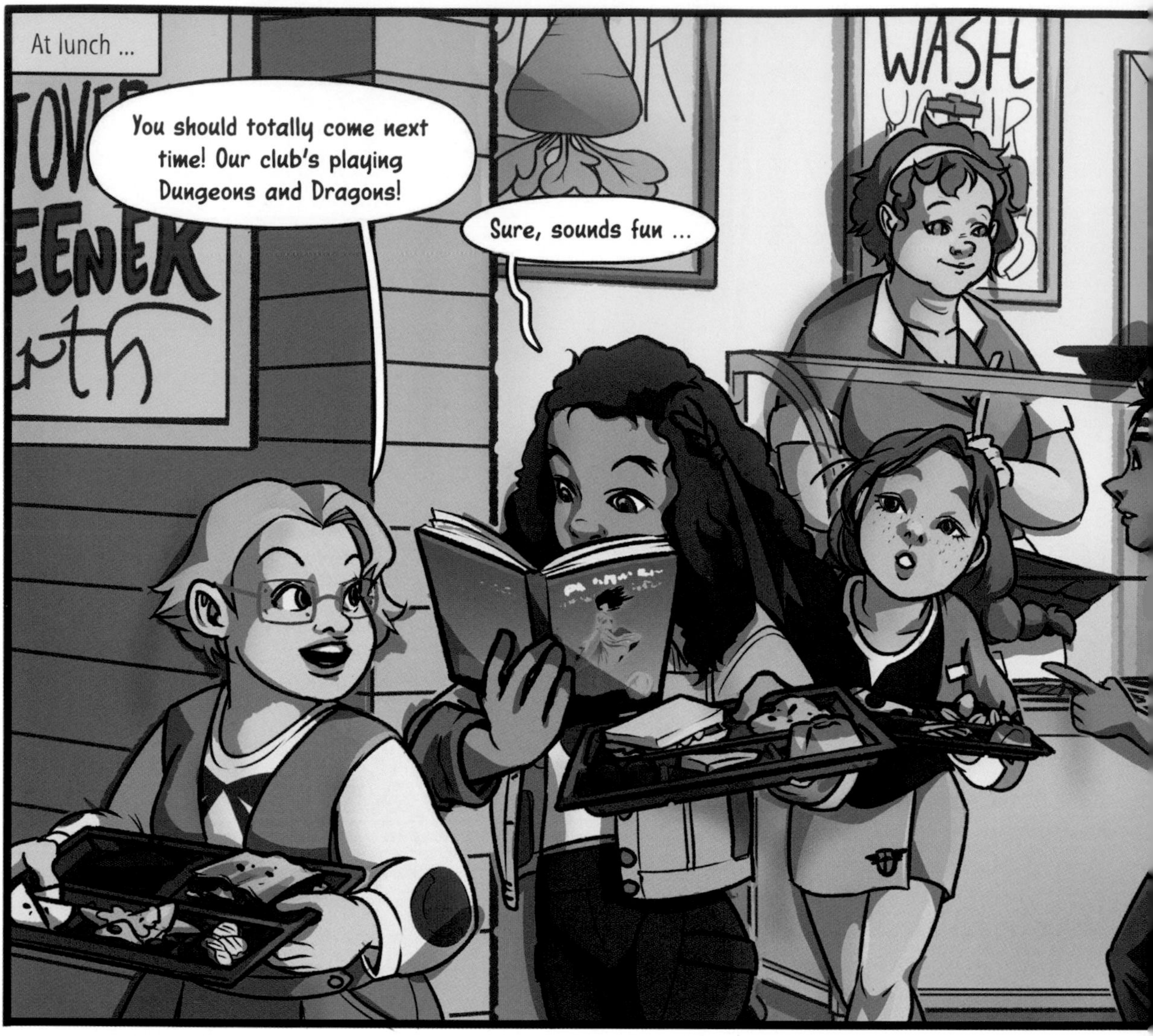
At lunch ...
WASH
You should totally come next time! Our club's playing Dungeons and Dragons!
Sure, sounds fun ...

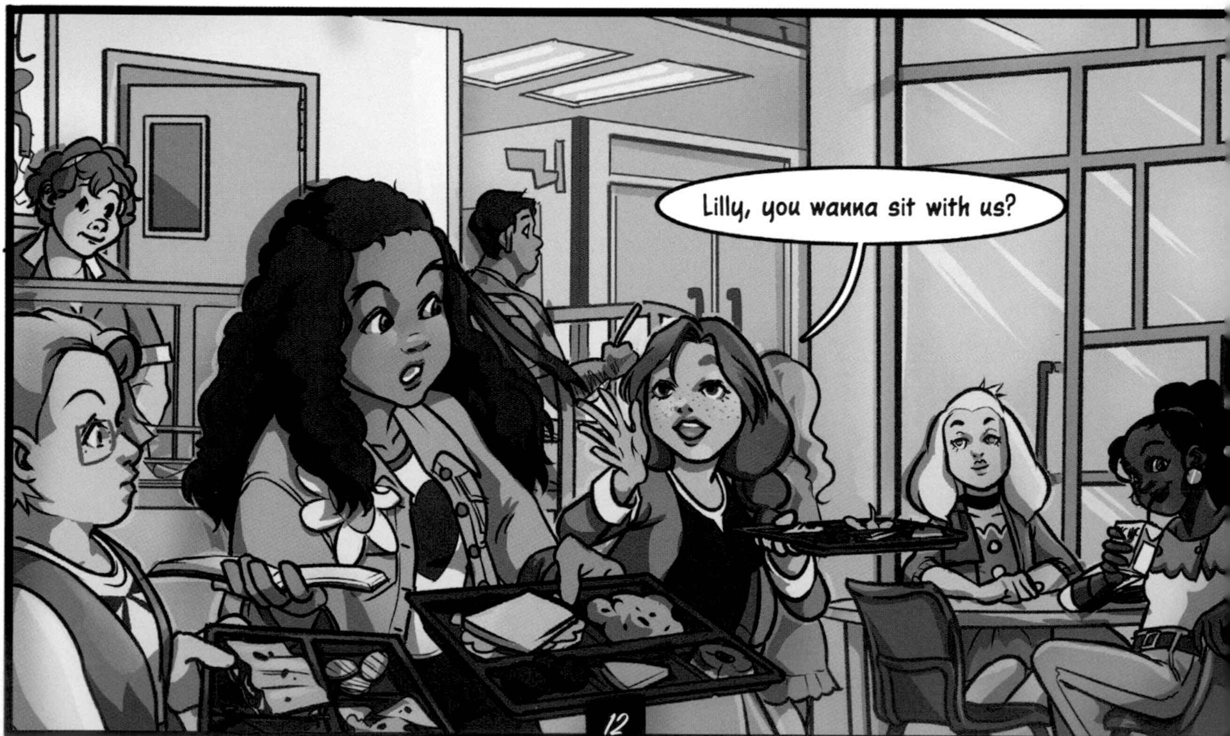
Lilly, you wanna sit with us?

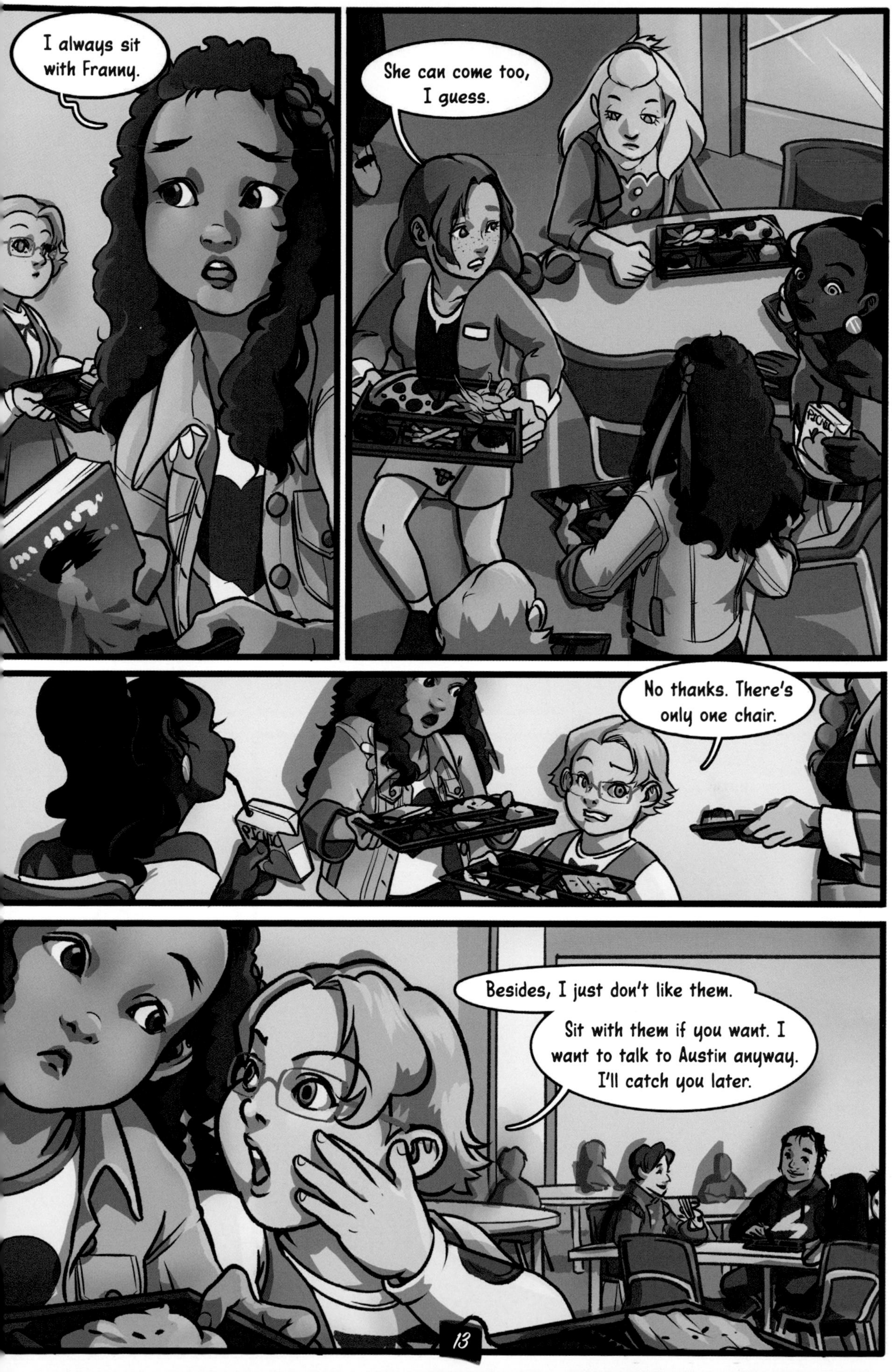
I always sit with Franny.
She can come too, I guess.
No thanks. There's only one chair.
Besides, I just don't like them.
Sit with them if you want. I want to talk to Austin anyway. I'll catch you later.

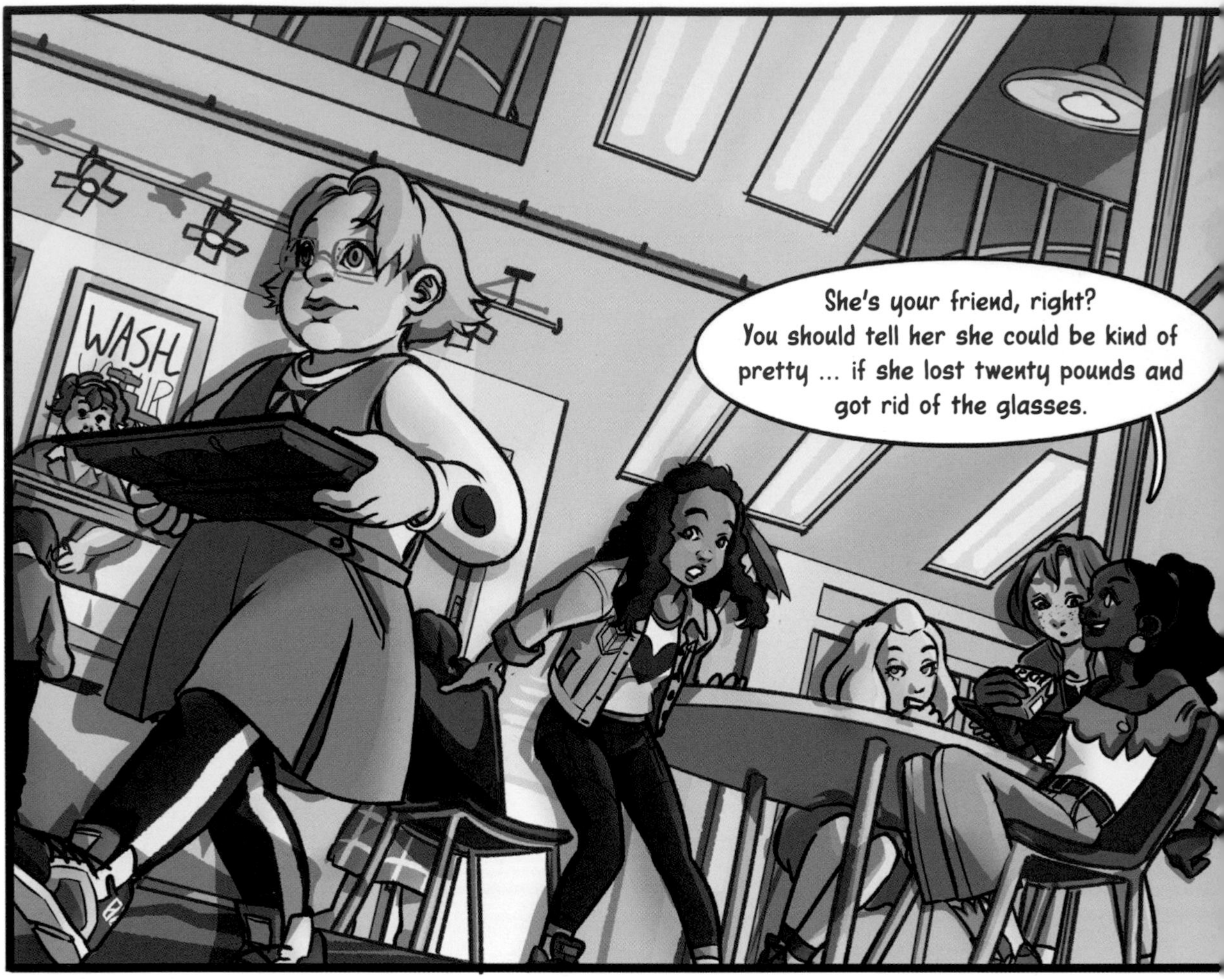
WASH
She's your friend, right? You should tell her she could be kind of pretty ... if she lost twenty pounds and got rid of the glasses.
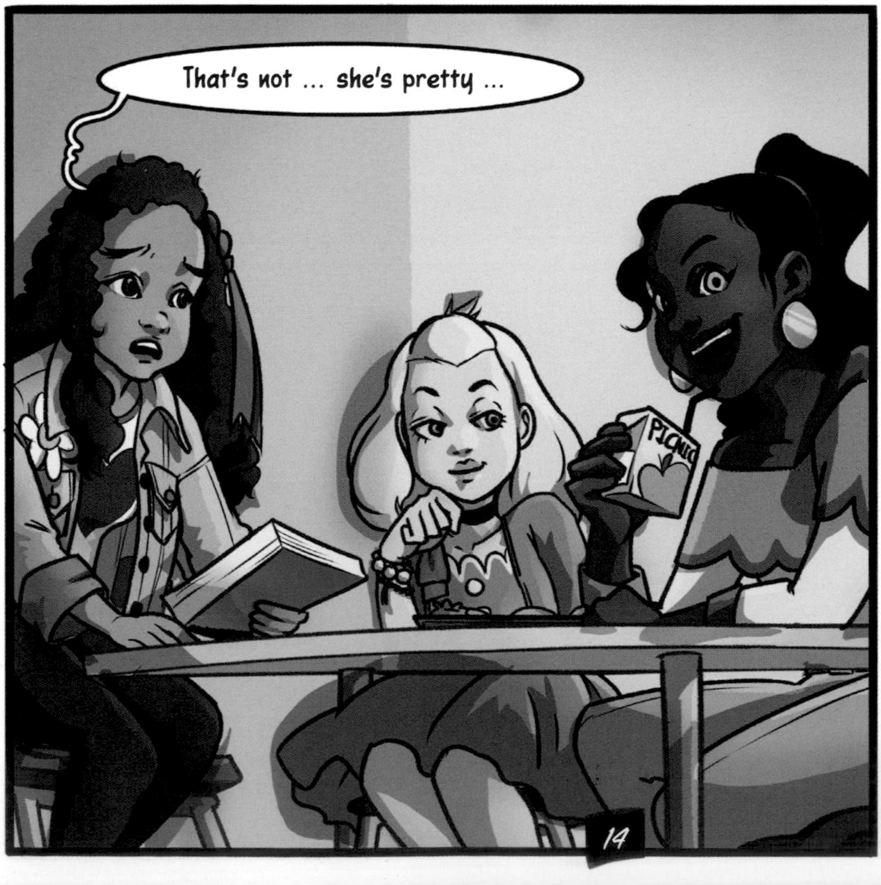
That's not ... she's pretty ...
PICNIC
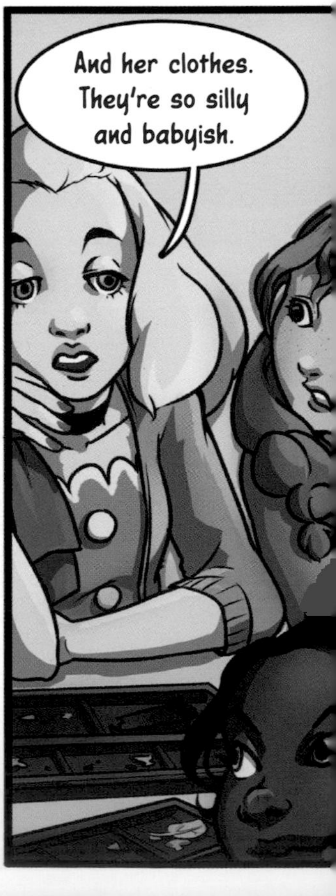
And her clothes. They're so silly and babyish.

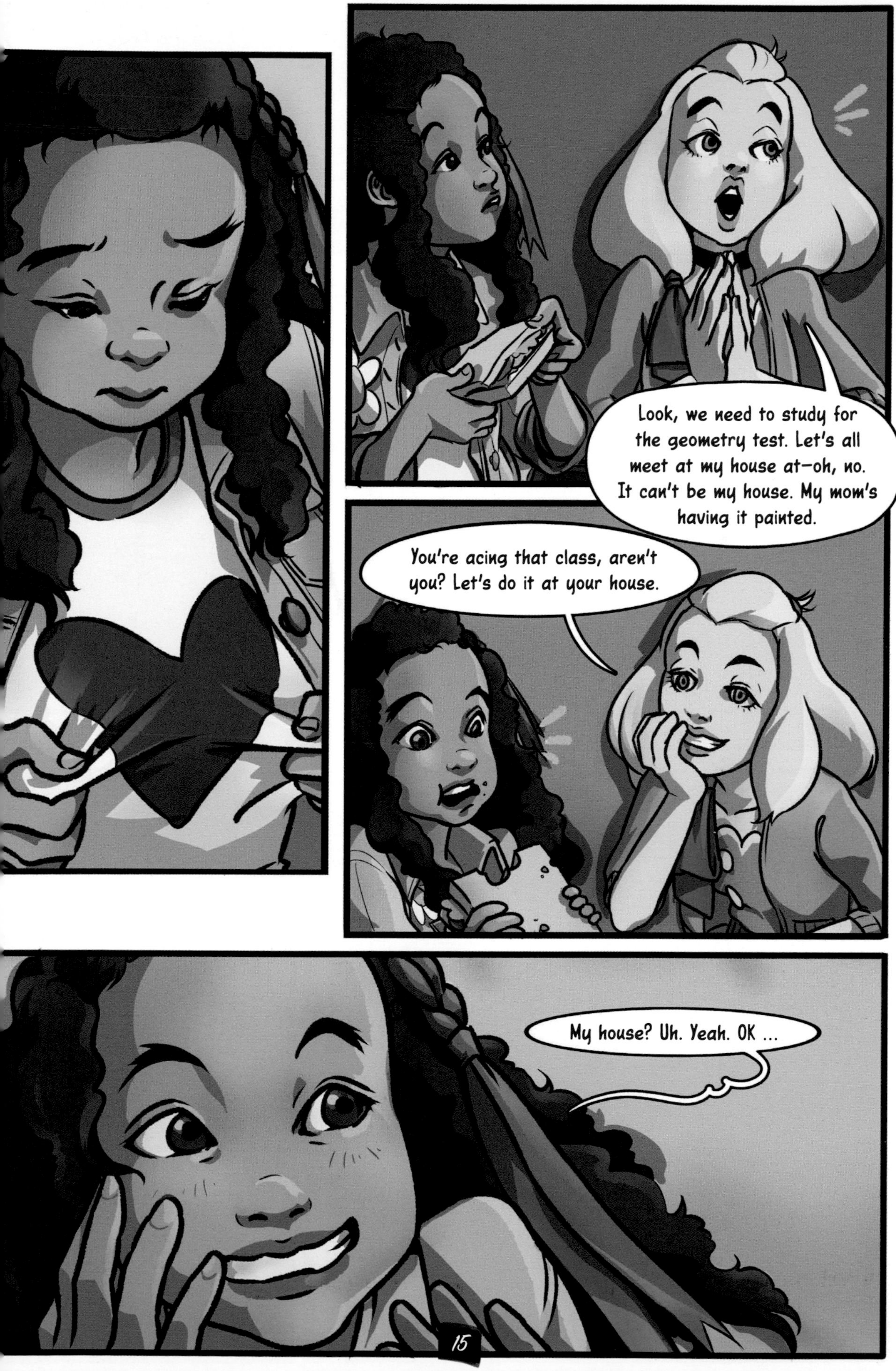
Look, we need to study for the geometry test. Let's all meet at my house at—oh, no. It can't be my house. My mom's having it painted.
You're acing that class, aren't you? Let's do it at your house.
My house? Uh. Yeah. OK ...

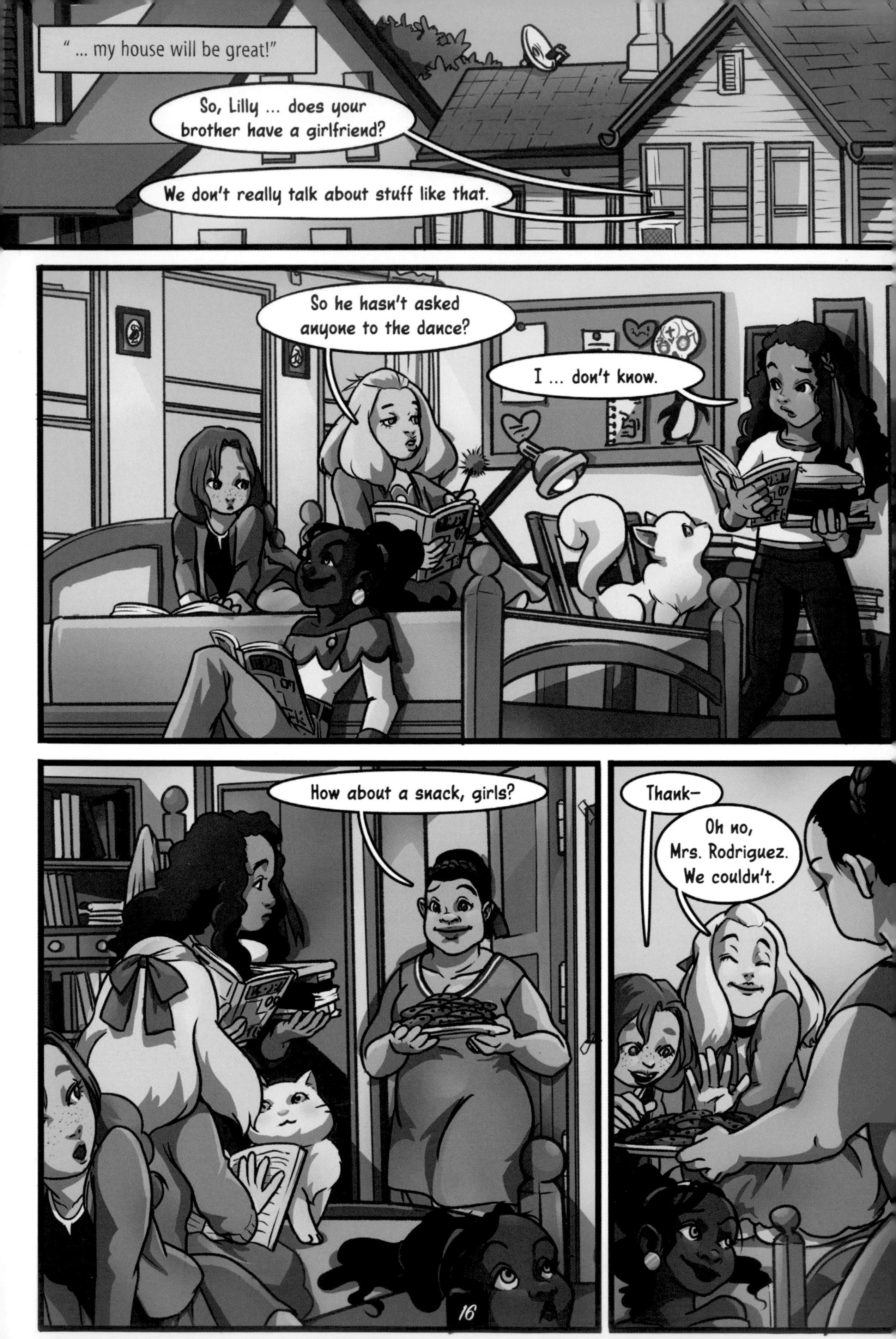
"... my house will be great!"
So, Lilly ... does your brother have a girlfriend?
We don't really talk about stuff like that.
So he hasn't asked anyone to the dance?
I ... don't know.
How about a snack, girls?
Thank—
Oh no, Mrs. Rodriguez. We couldn't.

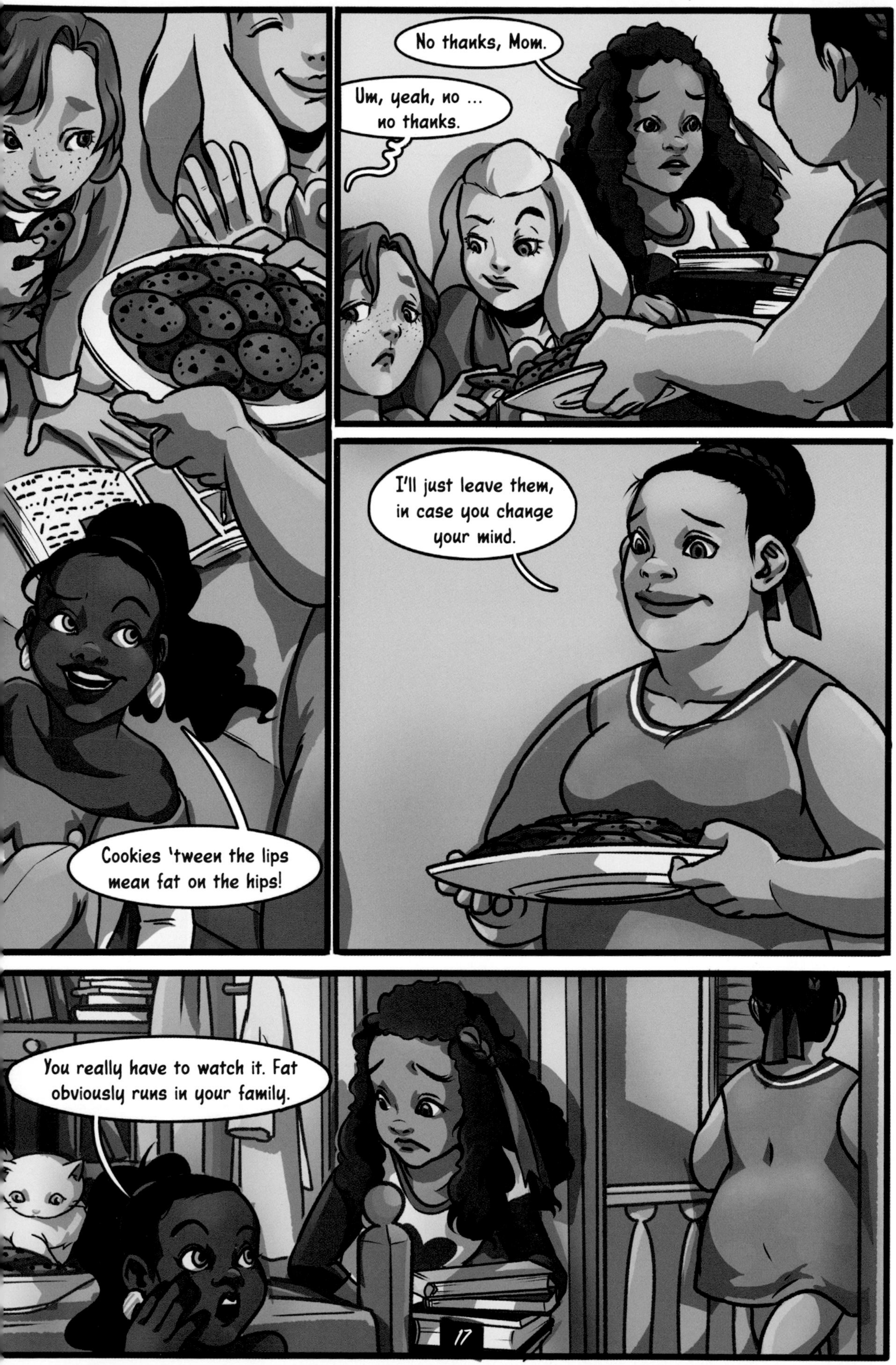
Cookies 'tween the lips mean fat on the hips!
No thanks, Mom.
Um, yeah, no ... no thanks.
I'll just leave them, in case you change your mind.
You really have to watch it. Fat obviously runs in your family.
17

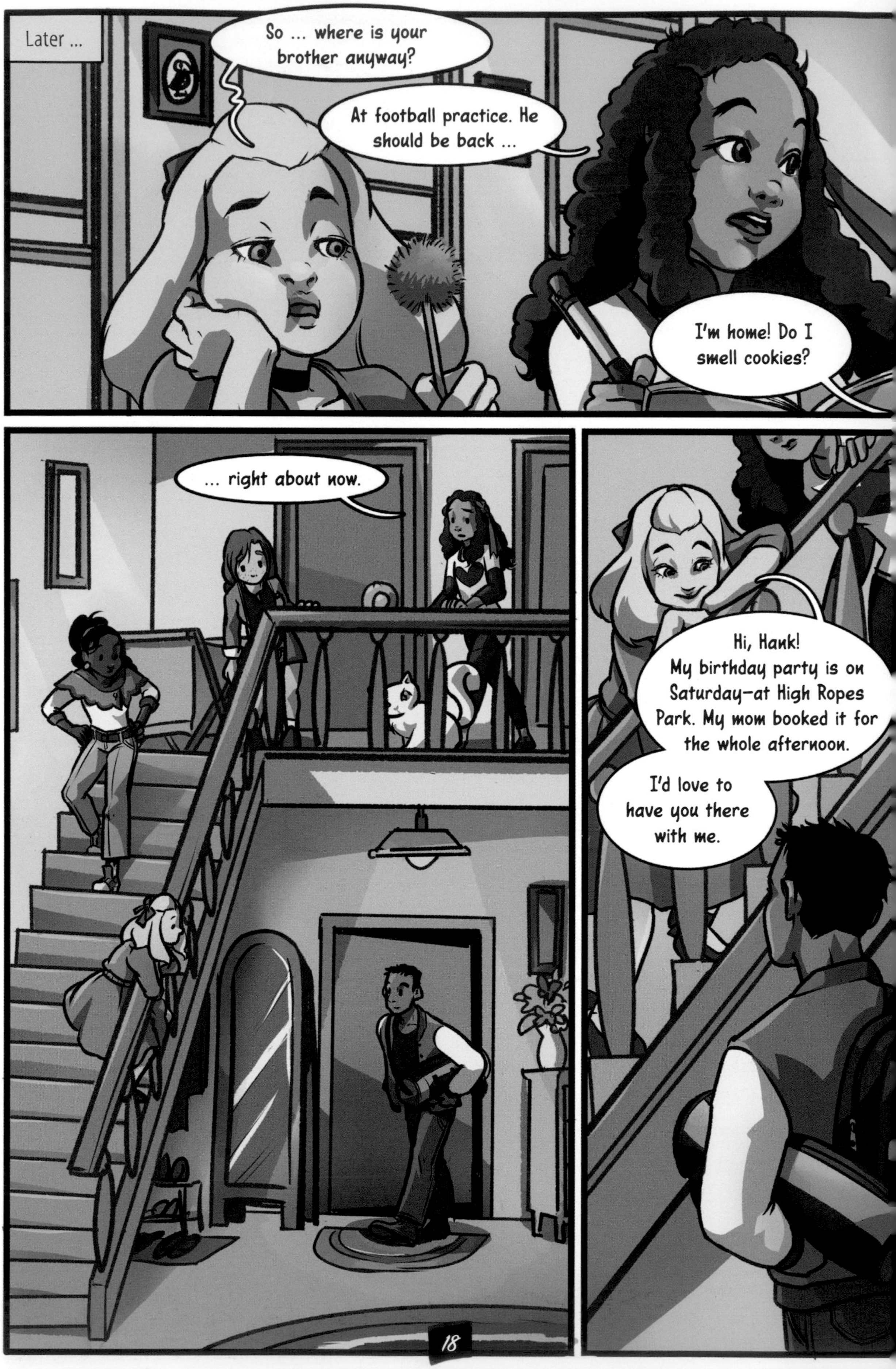
Later ...
So ... where is your brother anyway?
At football practice. He should be back ...
I'm home! Do I smell cookies?
... right about now.
Hi, Hank! My birthday party is on Saturday—at High Ropes Park. My mom booked it for the whole afternoon.
I'd love to have you there with me.

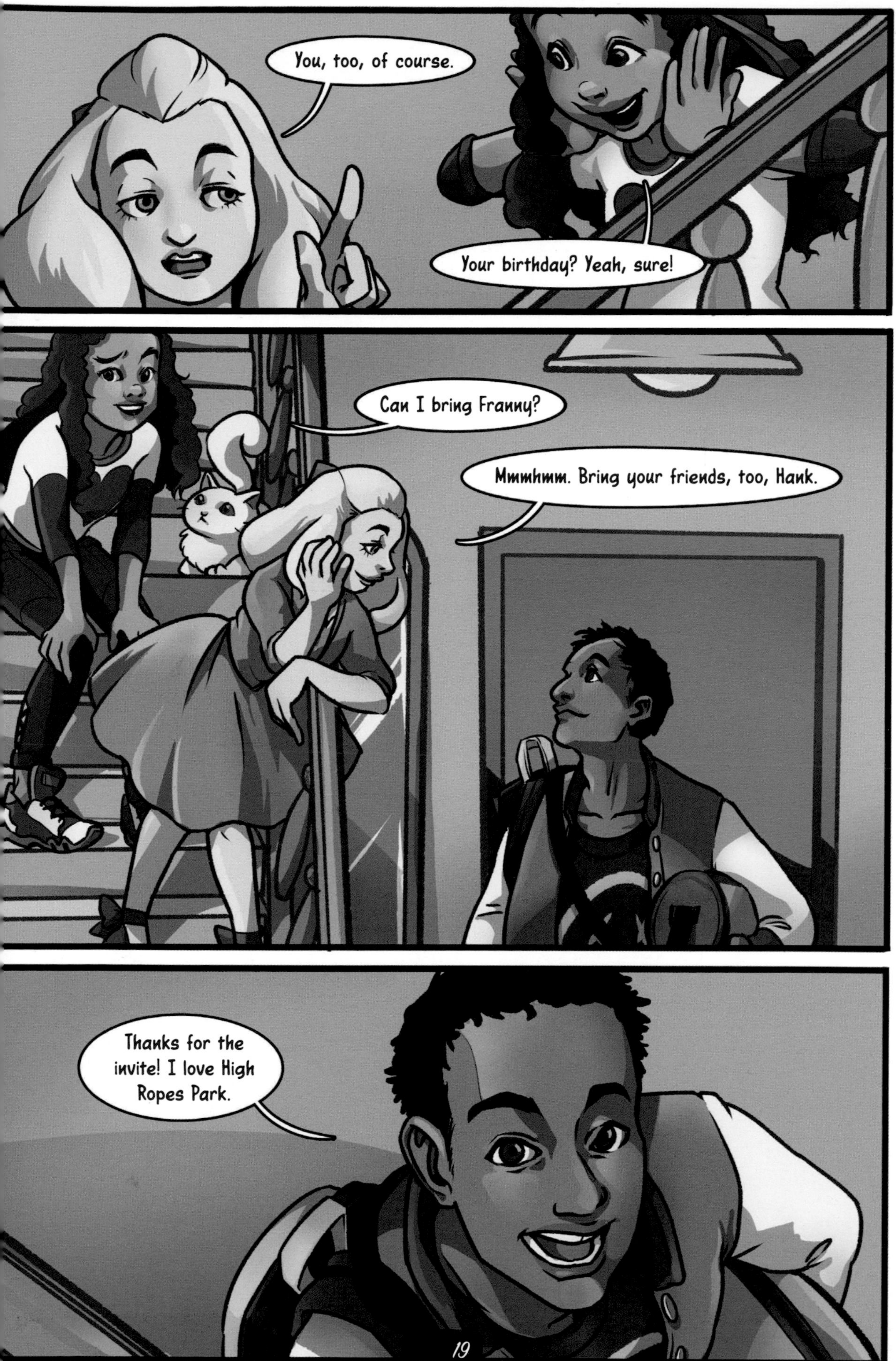
You, too, of course.
Your birthday? Yeah, sure!
Can I bring Franny?
Mmmhmm. Bring your friends, too, Hank.
Thanks for the invite! I love High Ropes Park.

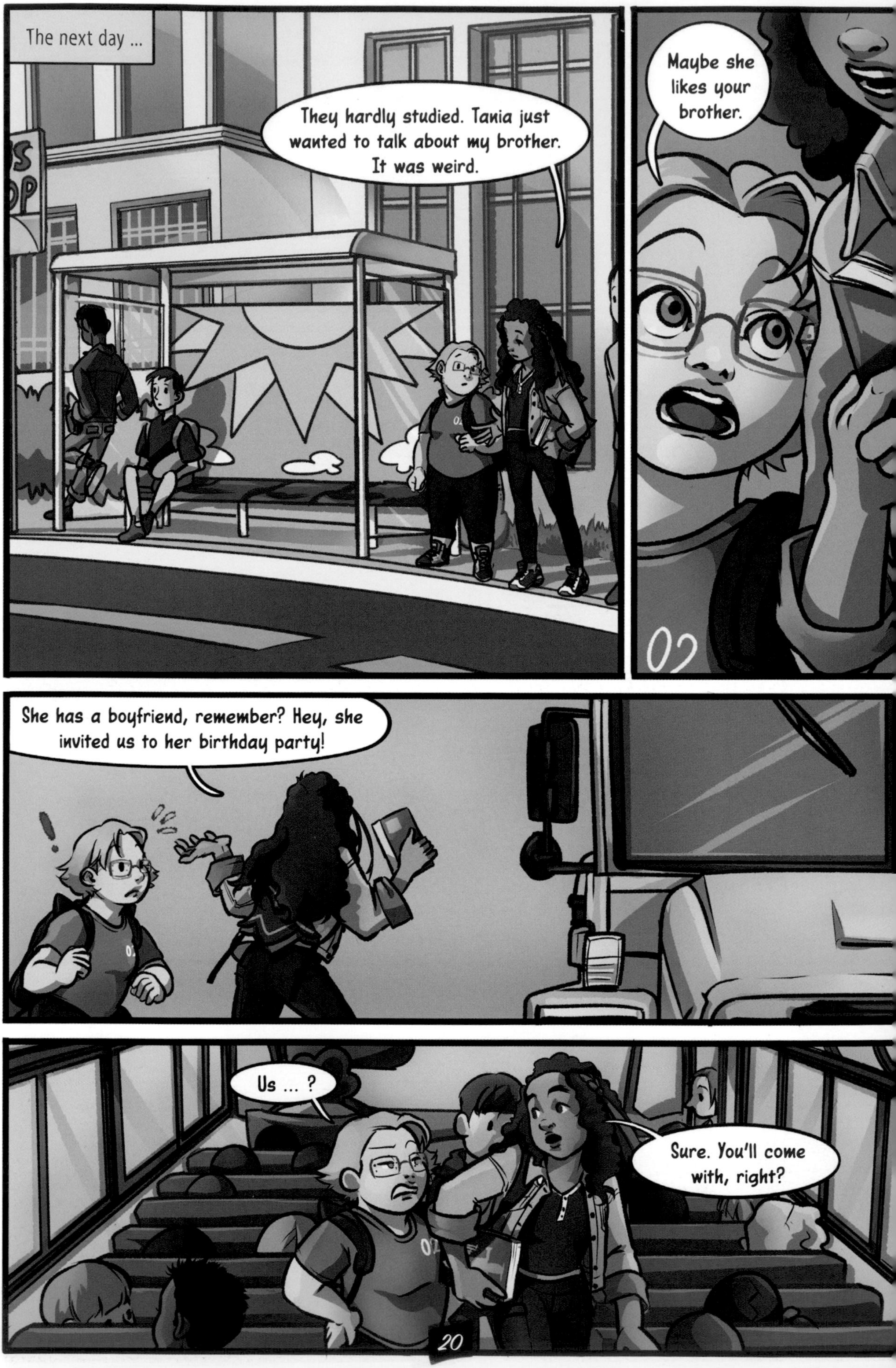

The next day ...
They hardly studied. Tania just wanted to talk about my brother. It was weird.
Maybe she likes your brother.
She has a boyfriend, remember? Hey, she invited us to her birthday party!
Us ... ?
Sure. You'll come with, right?

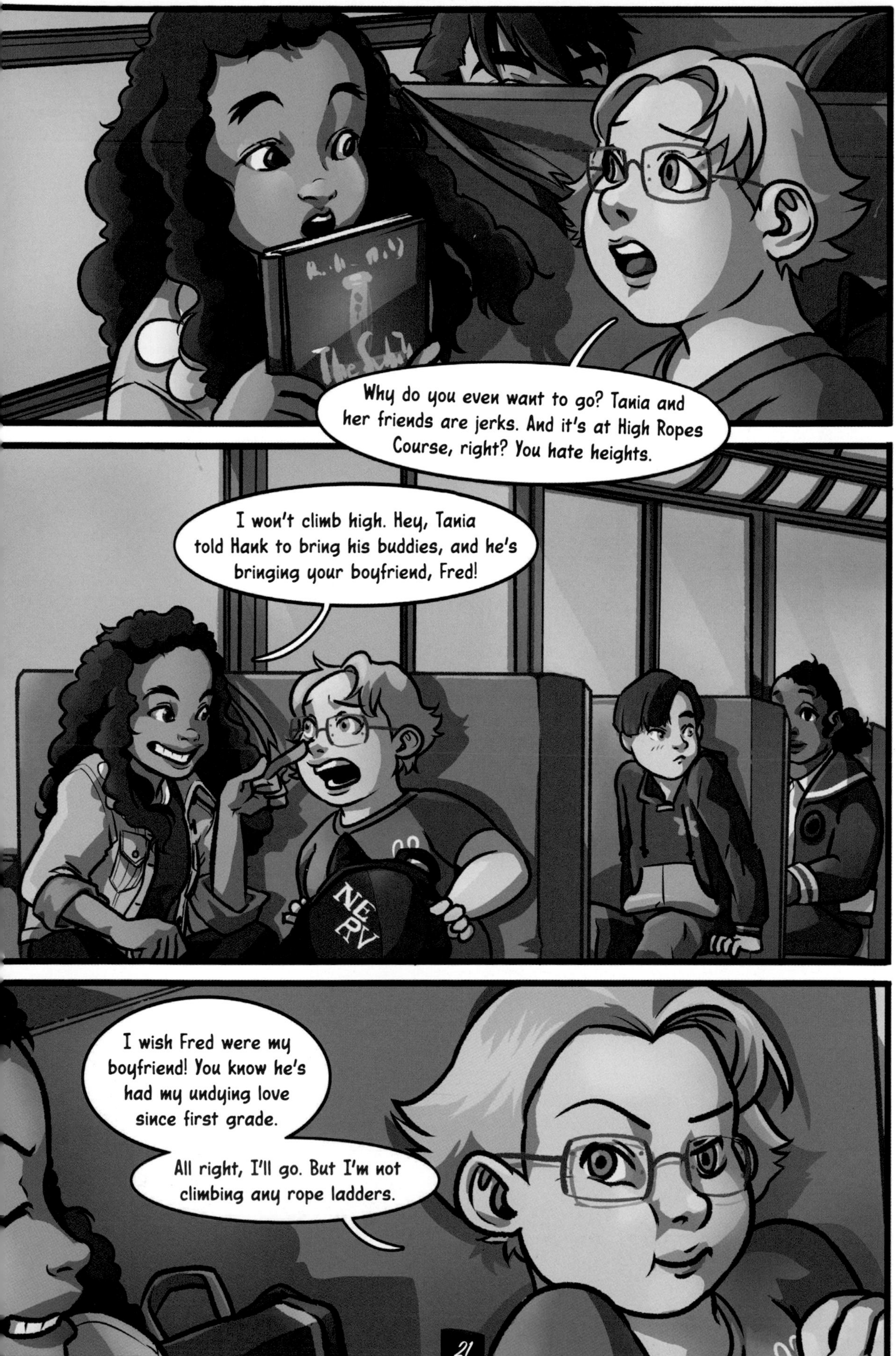
Why do you even want to go? Tania and her friends are jerks. And it's at High Ropes Course, right? You hate heights.
I won't climb high. Hey, Tania told Hank to bring his buddies, and he's bringing your boyfriend, Fred!
NE RV
I wish Fred were my boyfriend! You know he's had my undying love since first grade.
All right, I'll go. But I'm not climbing any rope ladders.

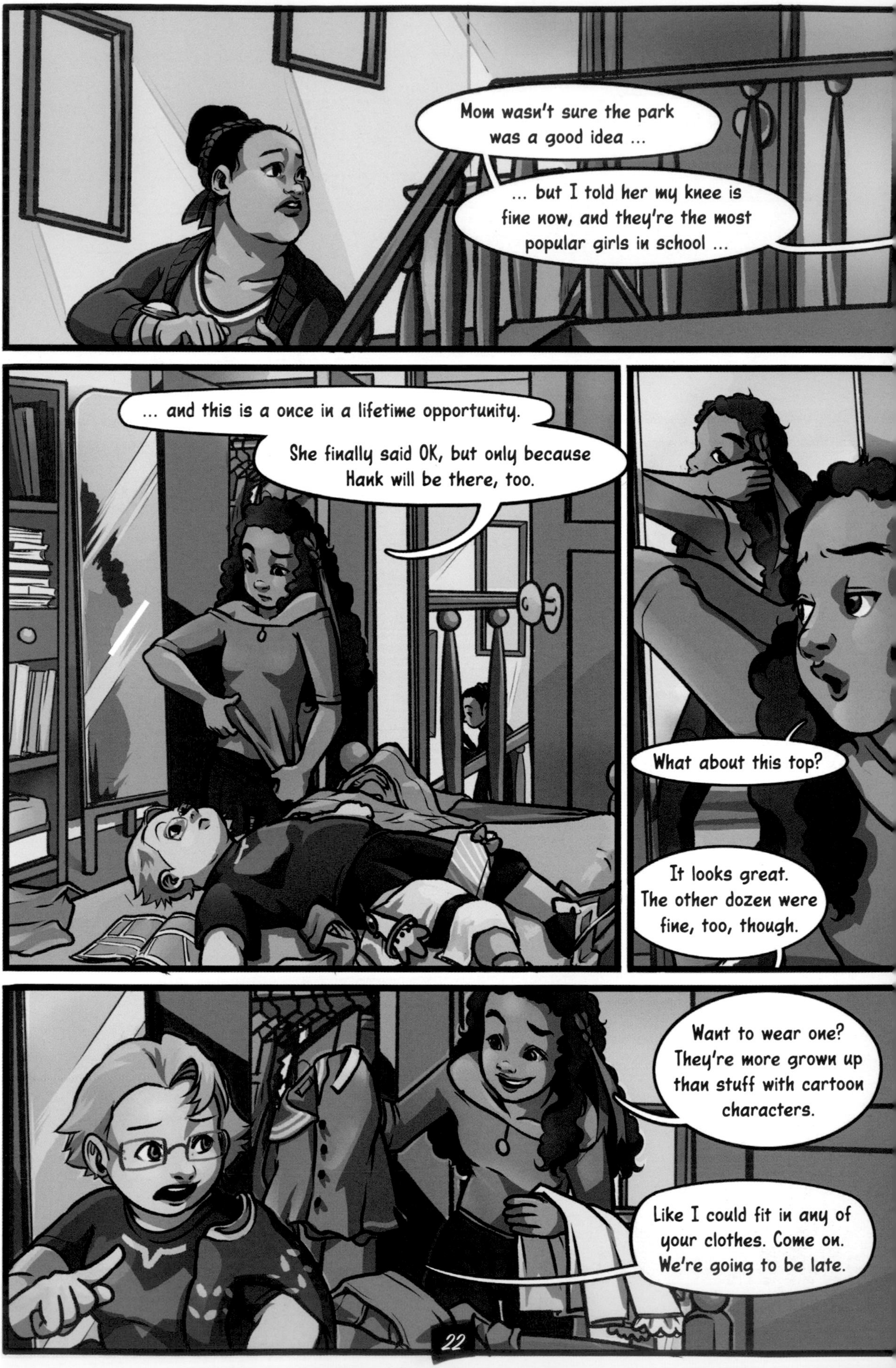
Mom wasn't sure the park was a good idea ...
... but I told her my knee is fine now, and they're the most popular girls in school ...
... and this is a once in a lifetime opportunity.
She finally said OK, but only because Hank will be there, too.
What about this top?
It looks great. The other dozen were fine, too, though.
Want to wear one? They're more grown up than stuff with cartoon characters.
Like I could fit in any of your clothes. Come on. We're going to be late.

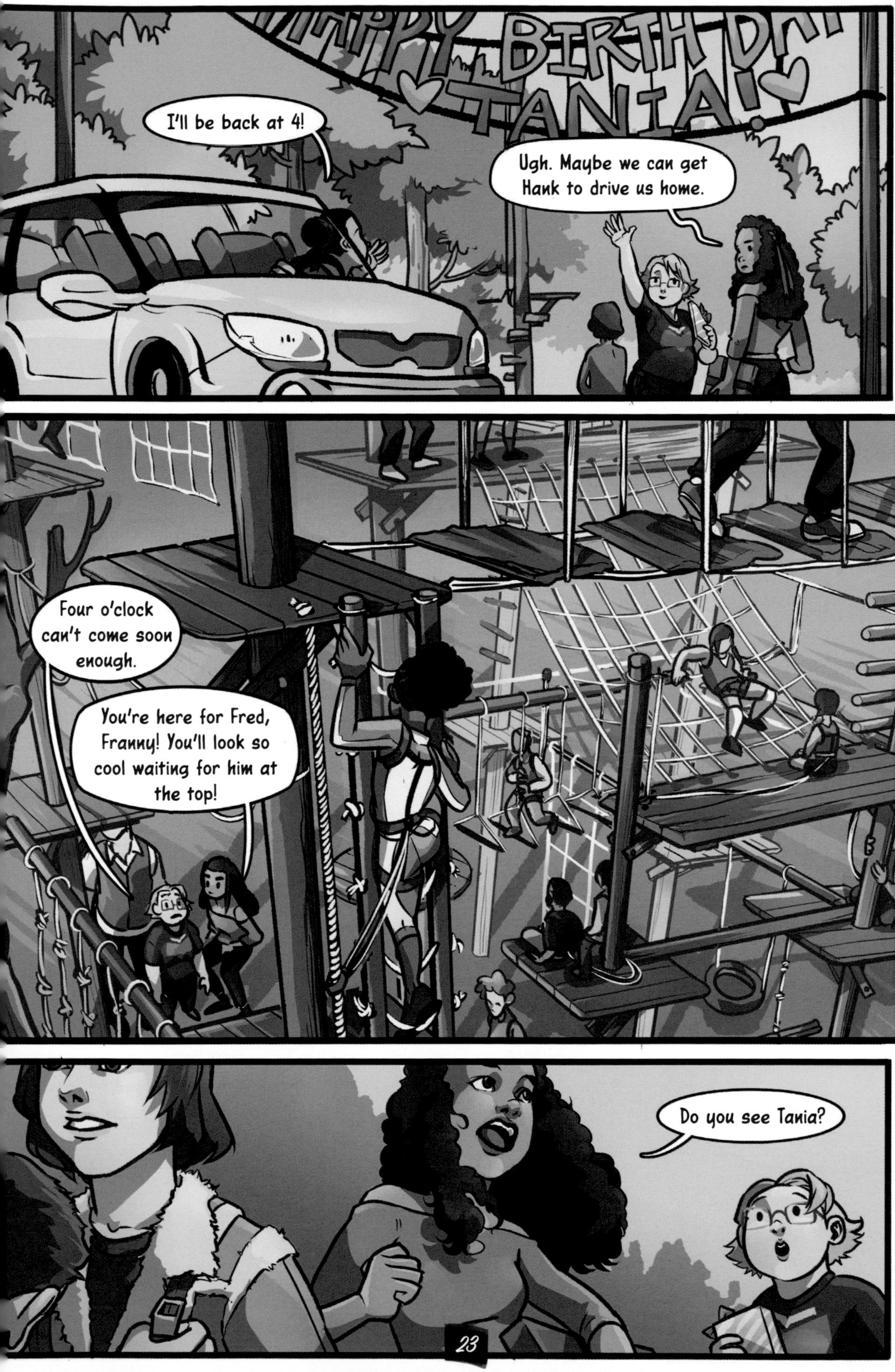
HAPPY BIRTHDAY TANIA!
I'll be back at 4!
Ugh. Maybe we can get Hank to drive us home.
Four o'clock can't come soon enough.
You're here for Fred, Franny! You'll look so cool waiting for him at the top!
Do you see Tania?

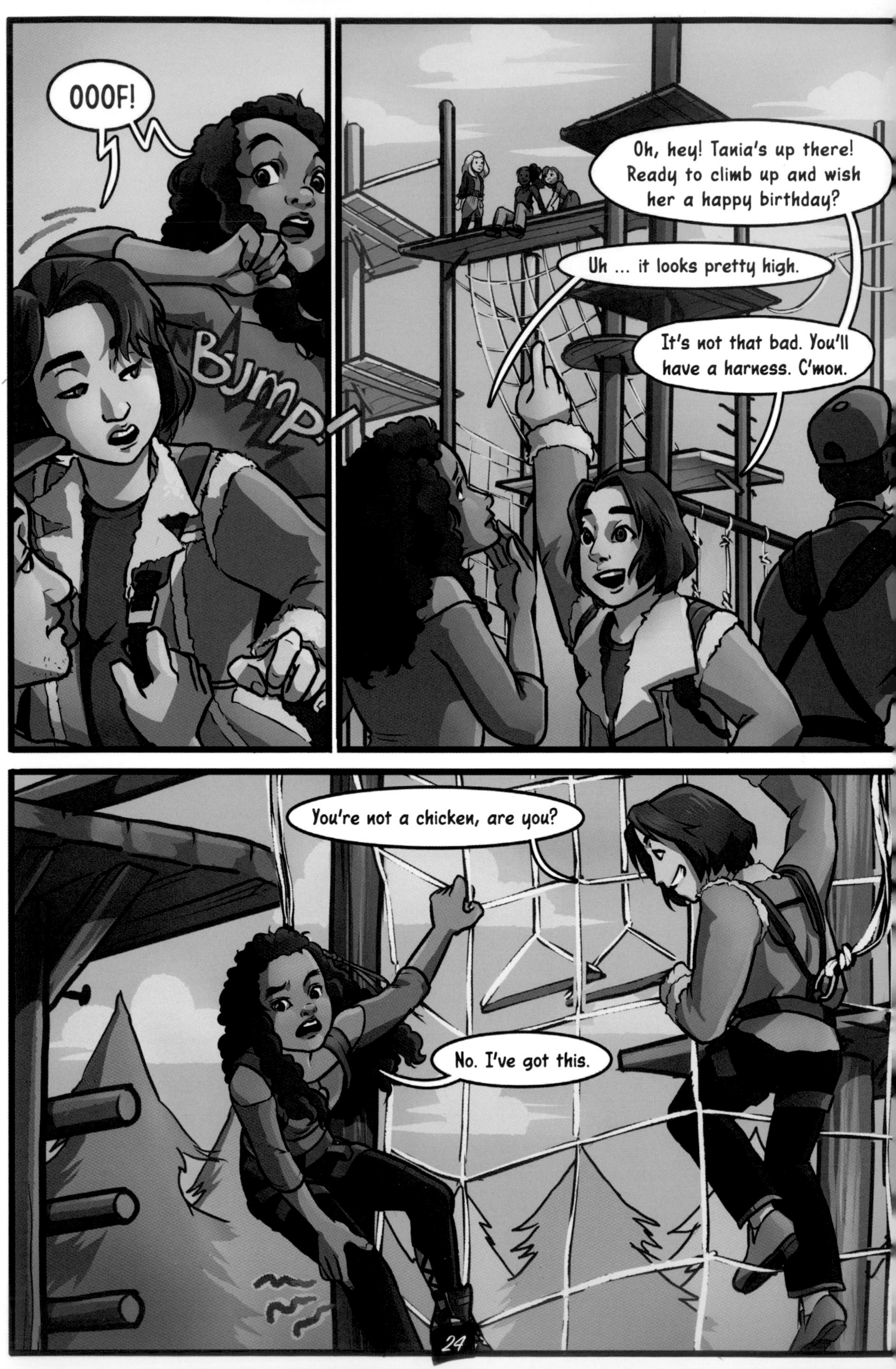
OOOF!
BUMP!
Oh, hey! Tania's up there! Ready to climb up and wish her a happy birthday?
Uh ... it looks pretty high.
It's not that bad. You'll have a harness. C'mon.
You're not a chicken, are you?
No. I've got this.

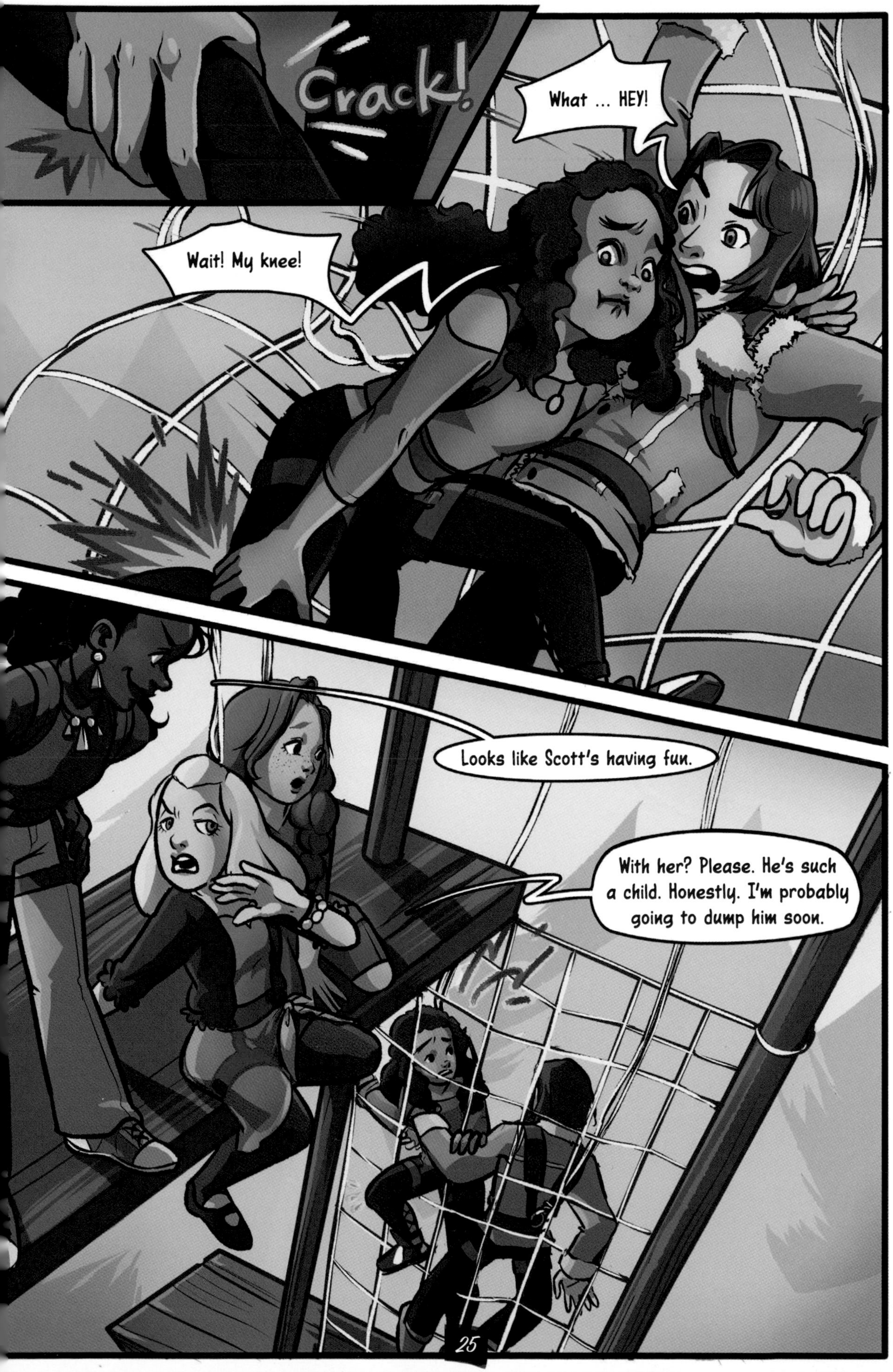
Crack!
What ... HEY!
Wait! My knee!
Looks like Scott's having fun.
With her? Please. He's such a child. Honestly. I'm probably going to dump him soon.

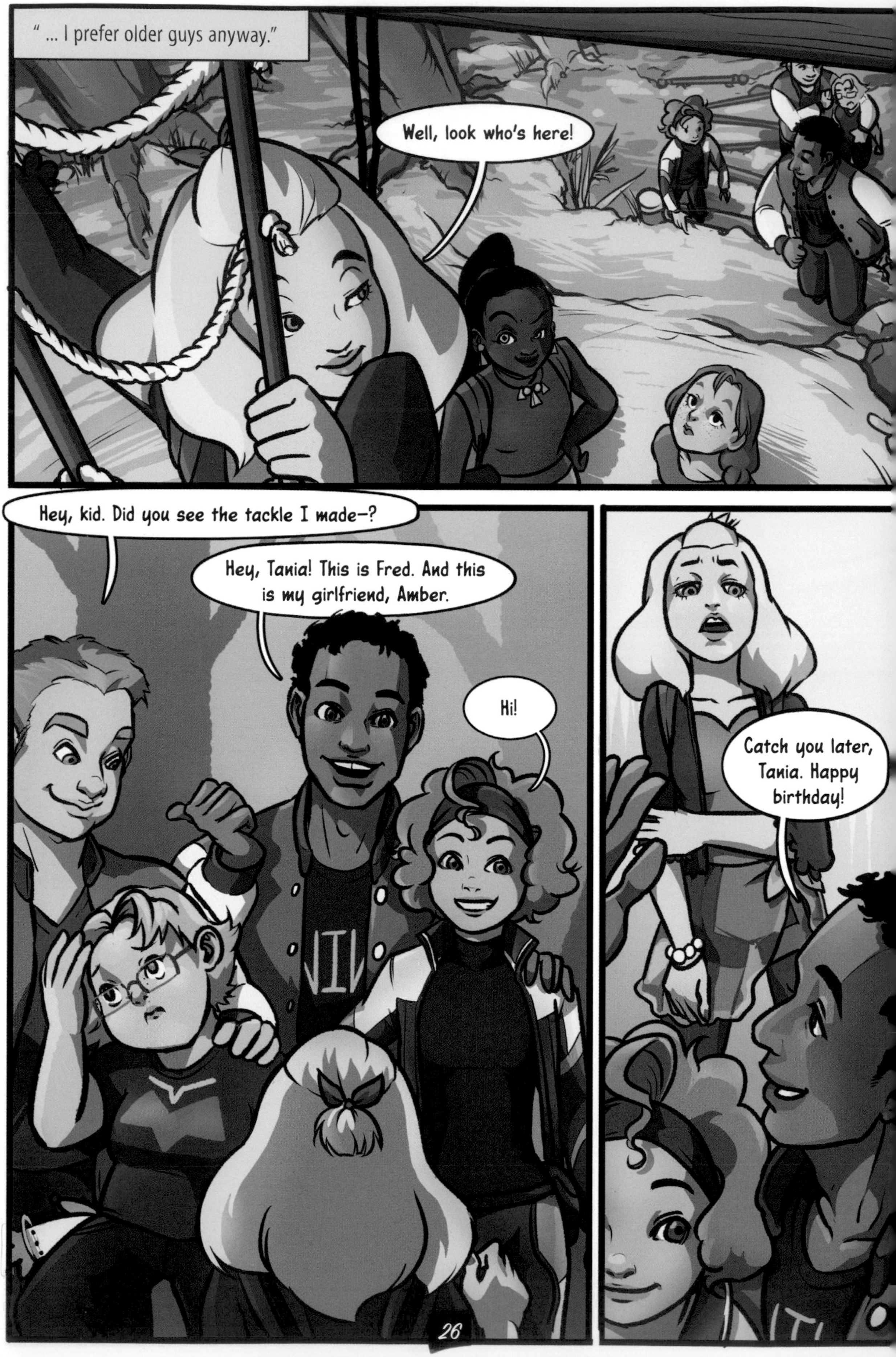
" ... I prefer older guys anyway."
Well, look who's here!
Hey, kid. Did you see the tackle I made—?
Hey, Tania! This is Fred. And this is my girlfriend, Amber.
Hi!
Catch you later, Tania. Happy birthday!

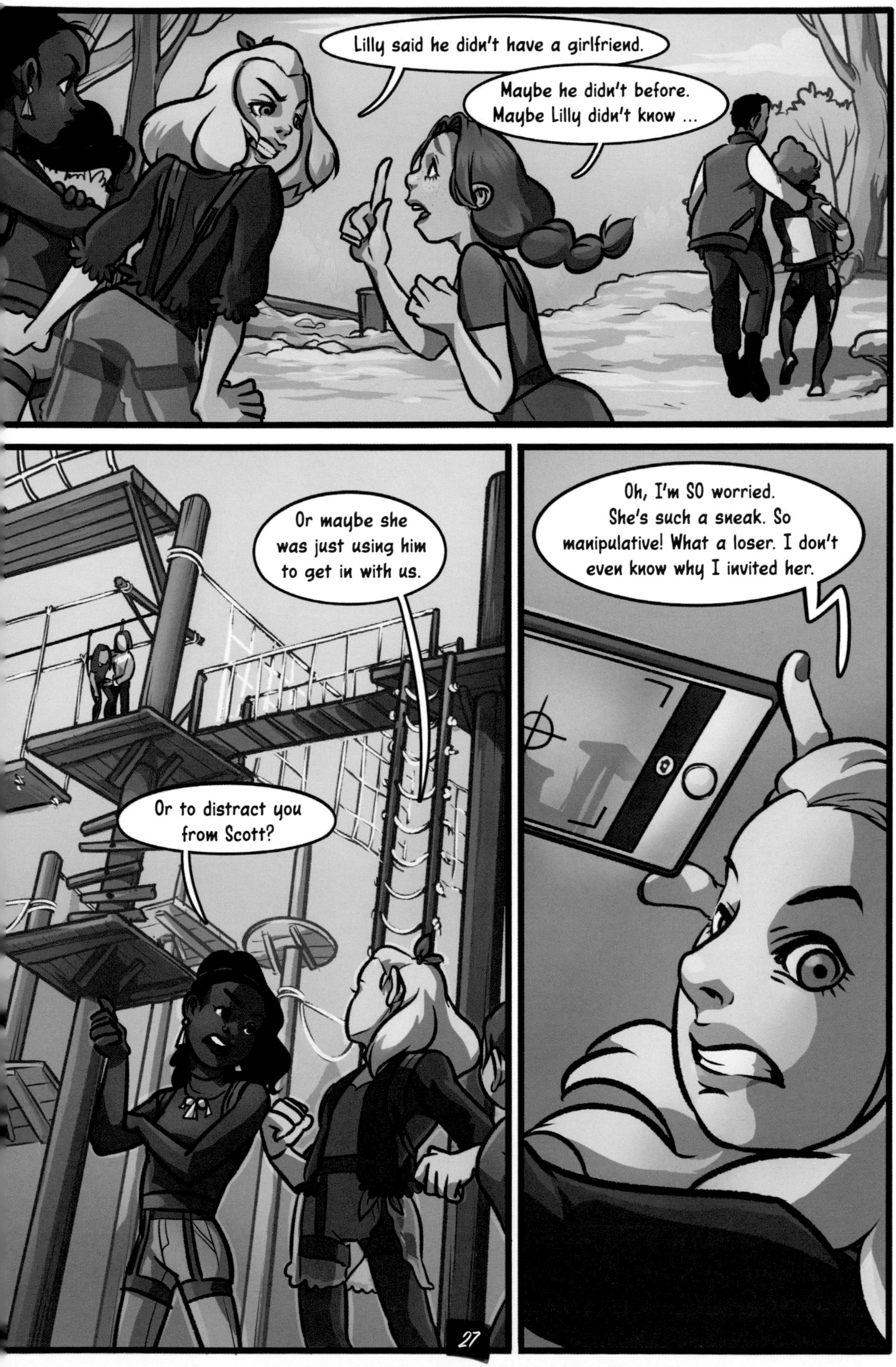
Lilly said he didn't have a girlfriend.
Maybe he didn't before. Maybe Lilly didn't know ...
Or maybe she was just using him to get in with us.
Or to distract you from Scott?
Oh, I'm SO worried. She's such a sneak. So manipulative! What a loser. I don't even know why I invited her.

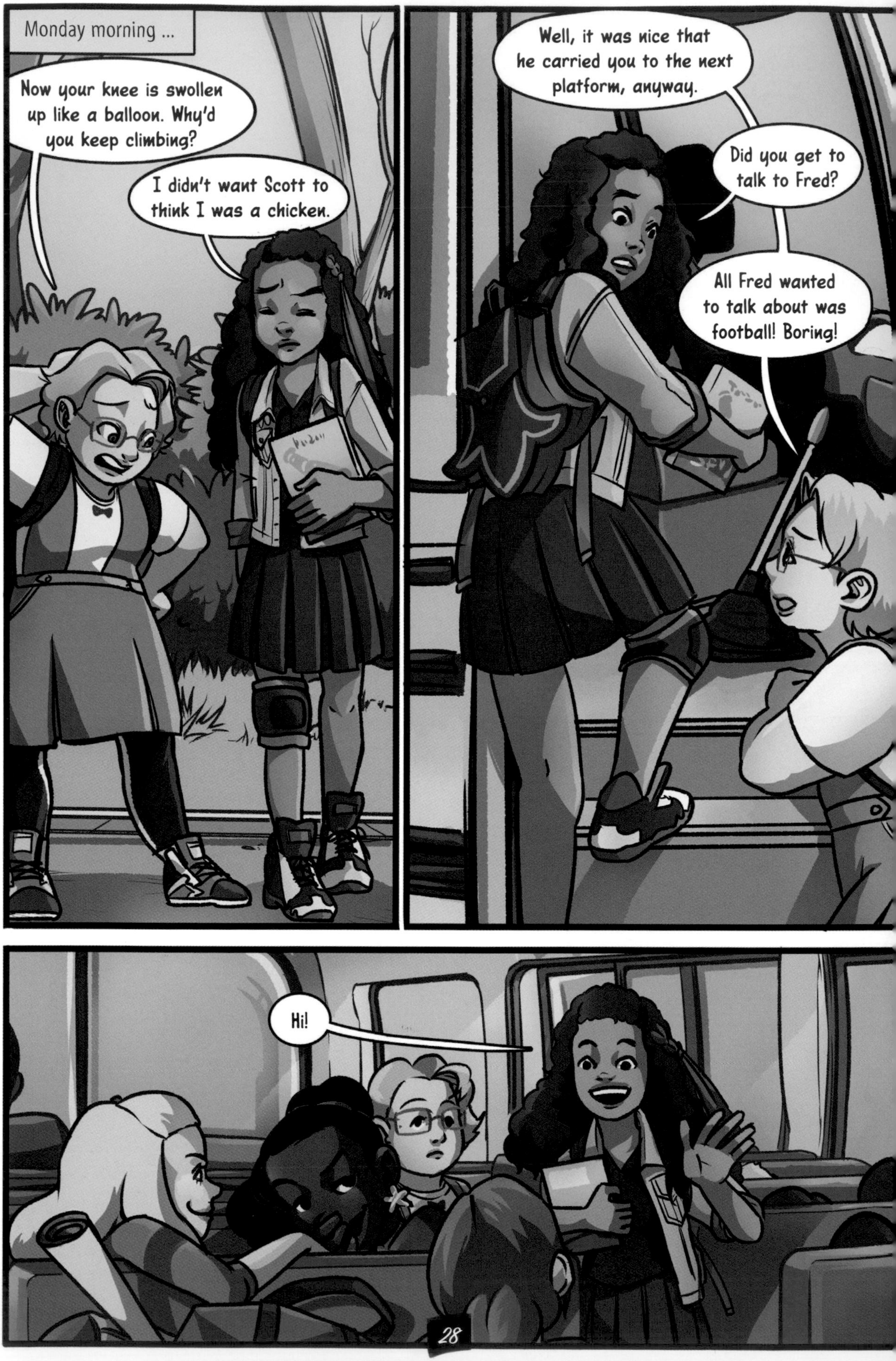
Monday morning ...
Now your knee is swollen up like a balloon. Why'd you keep climbing?
I didn't want Scott to think I was a chicken.
Well, it was nice that he carried you to the next platform, anyway.
Did you get to talk to Fred?
All Fred wanted to talk about was football! Boring!
Hi!

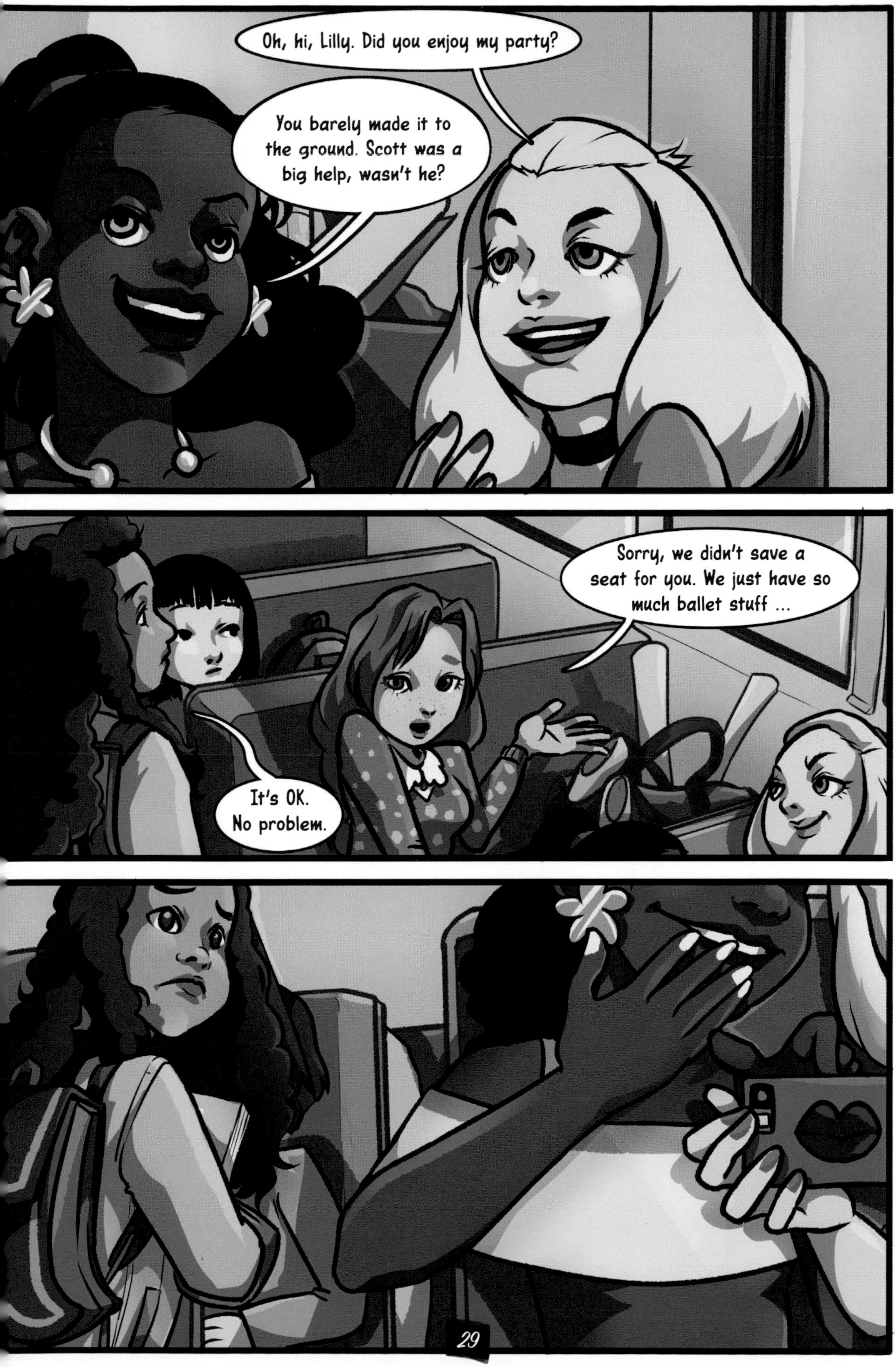

Oh, hi, Lilly. Did you enjoy my party?
You barely made it to the ground. Scott was a big help, wasn't he?
Sorry, we didn't save a seat for you. We just have so much ballet stuff ...
It's OK. No problem.

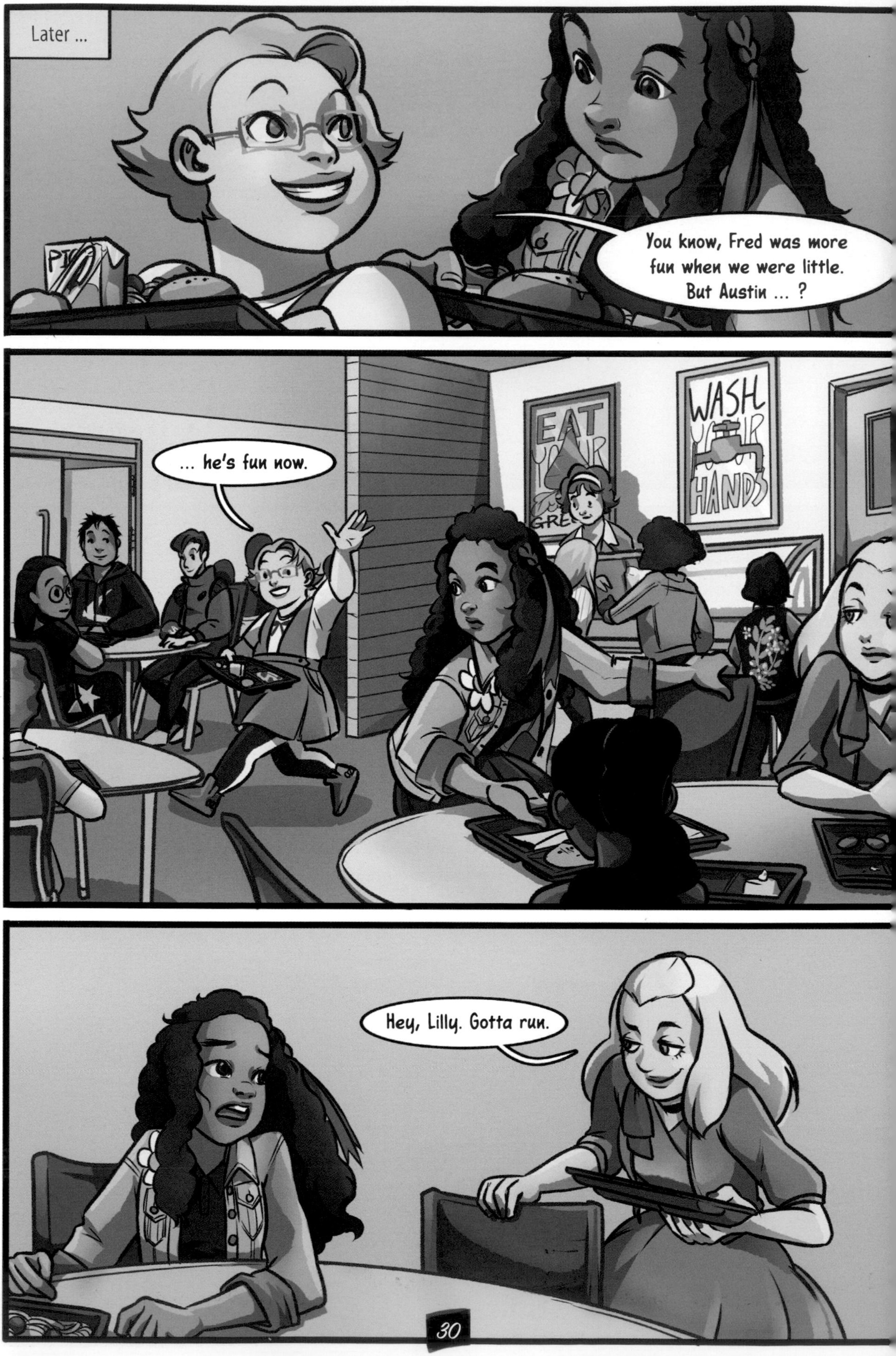
Later ...
You know, Fred was more fun when we were little. But Austin ... ?
... he's fun now.
EAT
WASH
HANDS
Hey, Lilly. Gotta run.

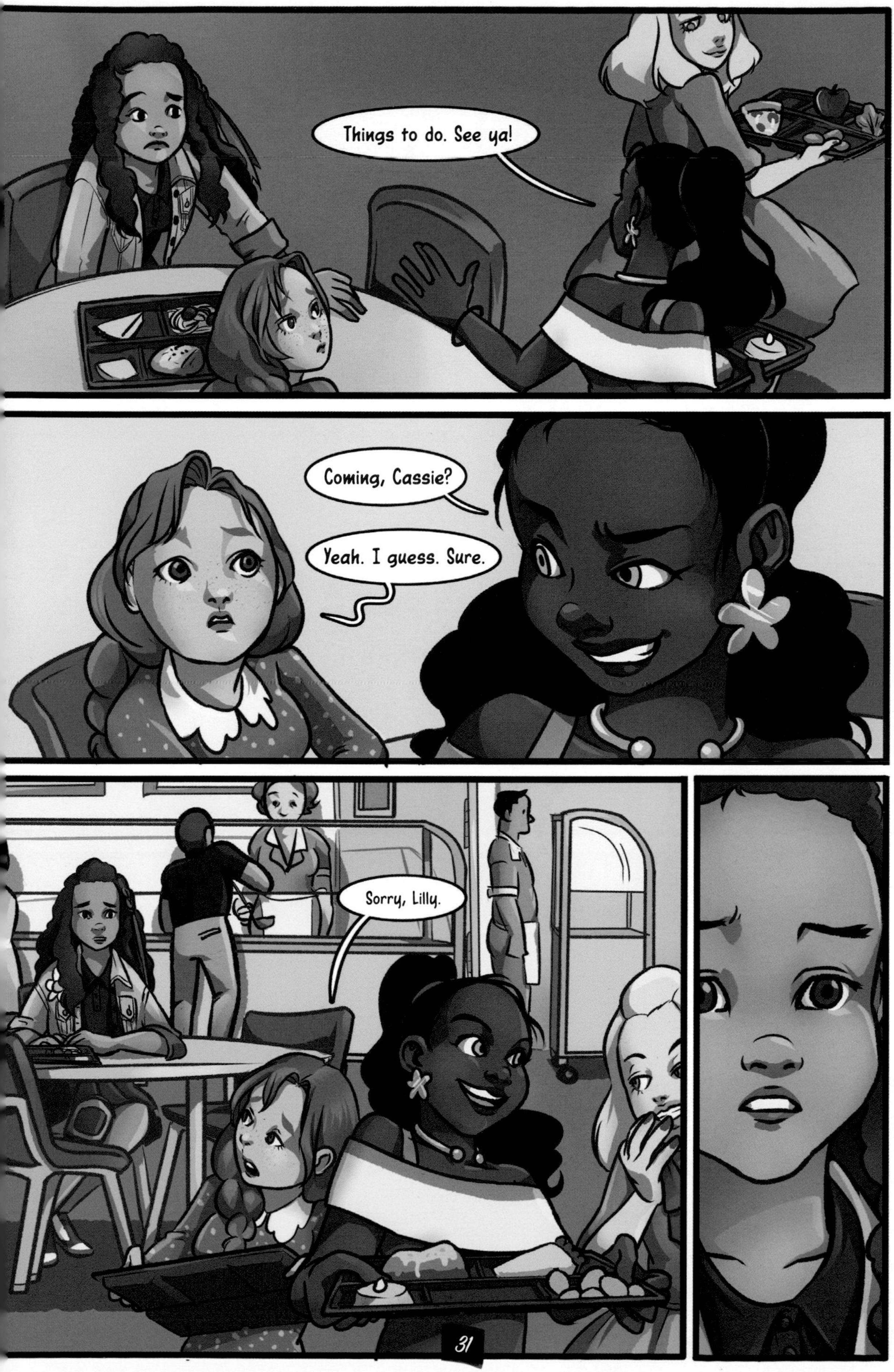
Things to do. See ya!
Coming, Cassie?
Yeah. I guess. Sure.
Sorry, Lilly.

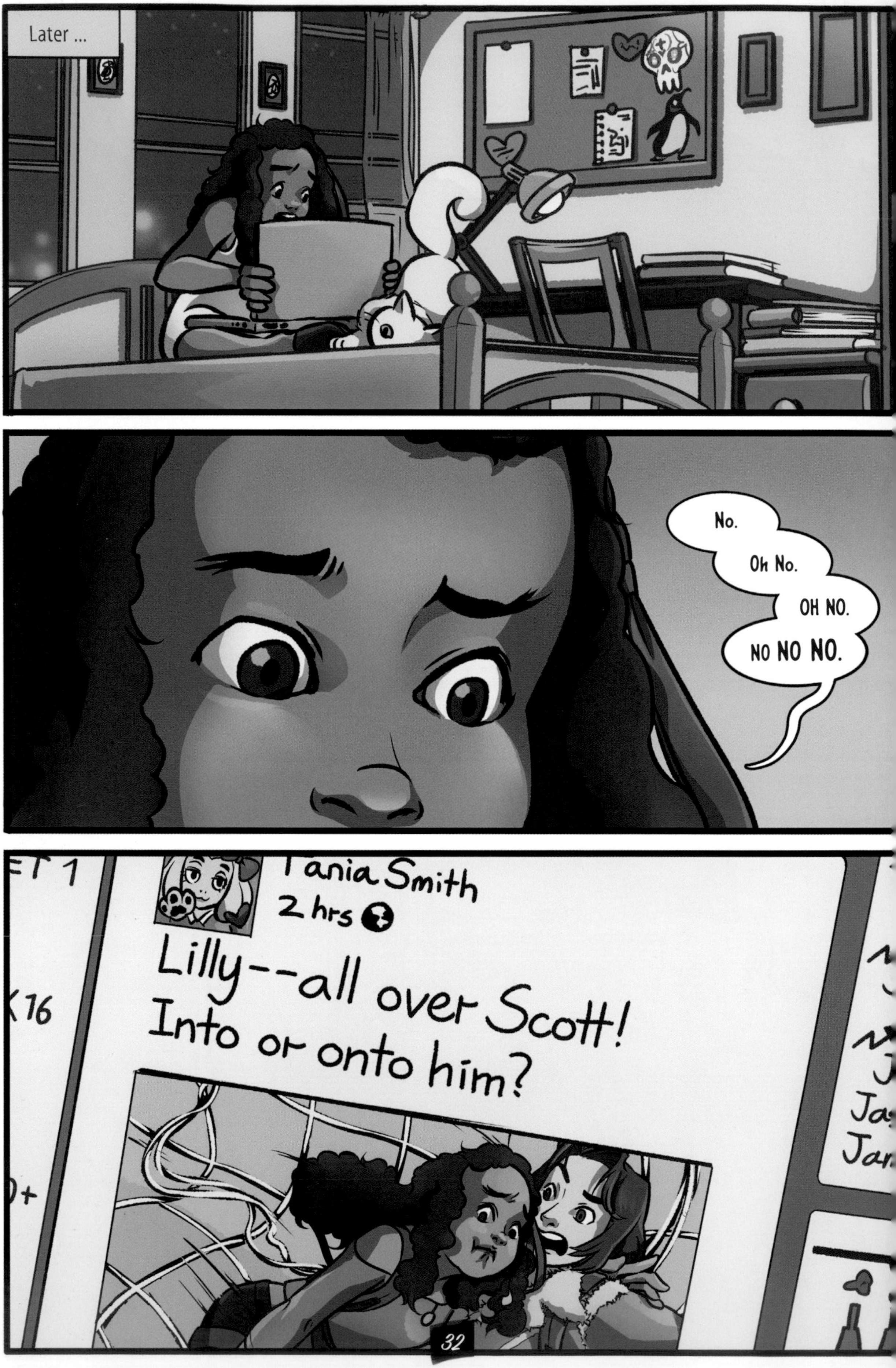
Later ...
No.
Oh No.
OH NO.
NO NO NO.
Tania Smith
2 hrs
Lilly--all over Scott! Into or onto him?

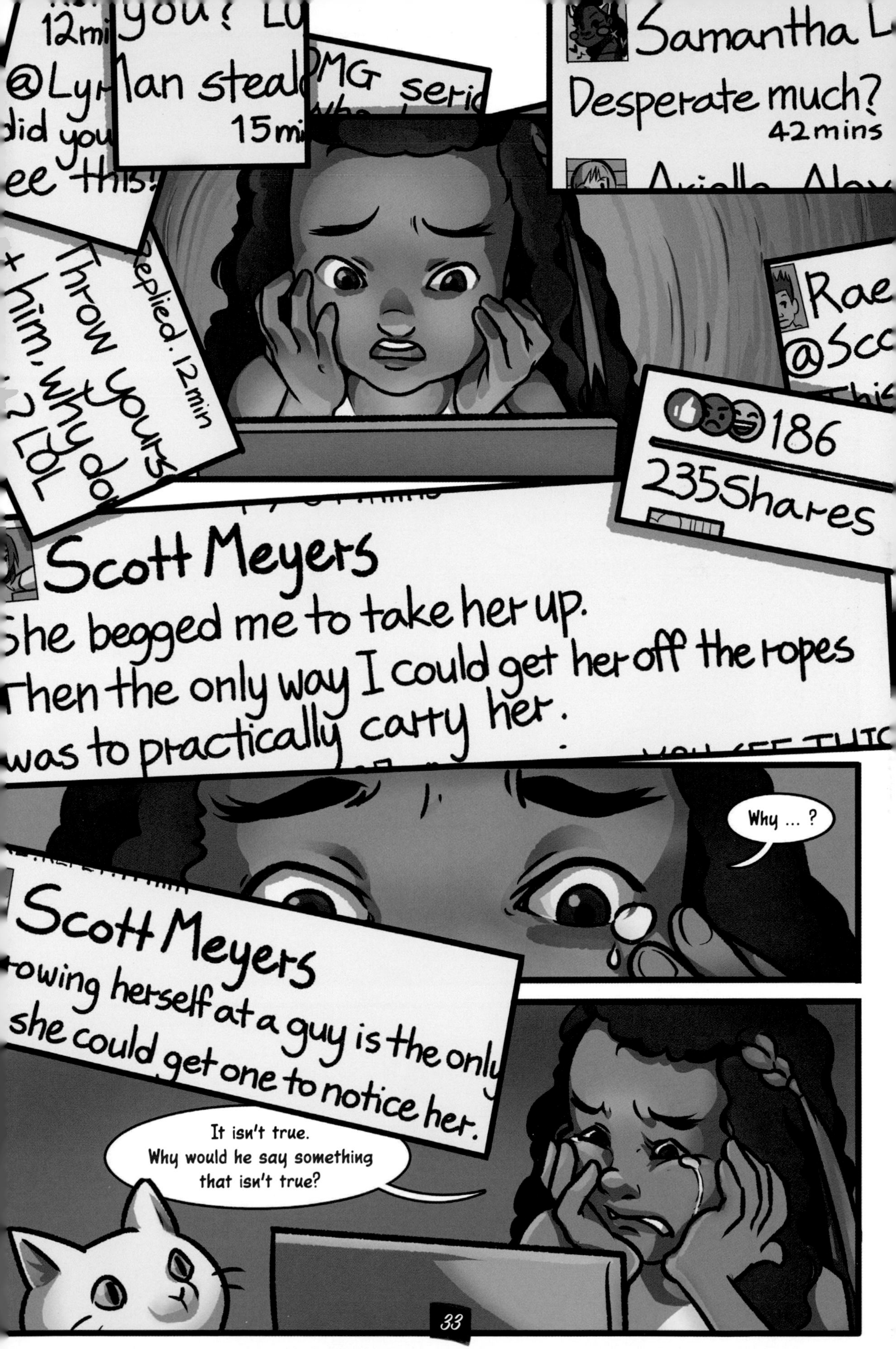

12mi
@Lyr
did you
ee this!
you? Ly
lan steal
15 mi
OMG seri
Samantha L
Desperate much?
42 mins
Replied. 12min
Throw yours
+ him, why do
? LOL
Rae
@Sco
186
235Shares
Scott Meyers
he begged me to take her up.
hen the only way I could get her off the ropes
was to practically carry her.
Why ... ?
Scott Meyers
rowing herself at a guy is the only
she could get one to notice her.
It isn't true.
Why would he say something
that isn't true?

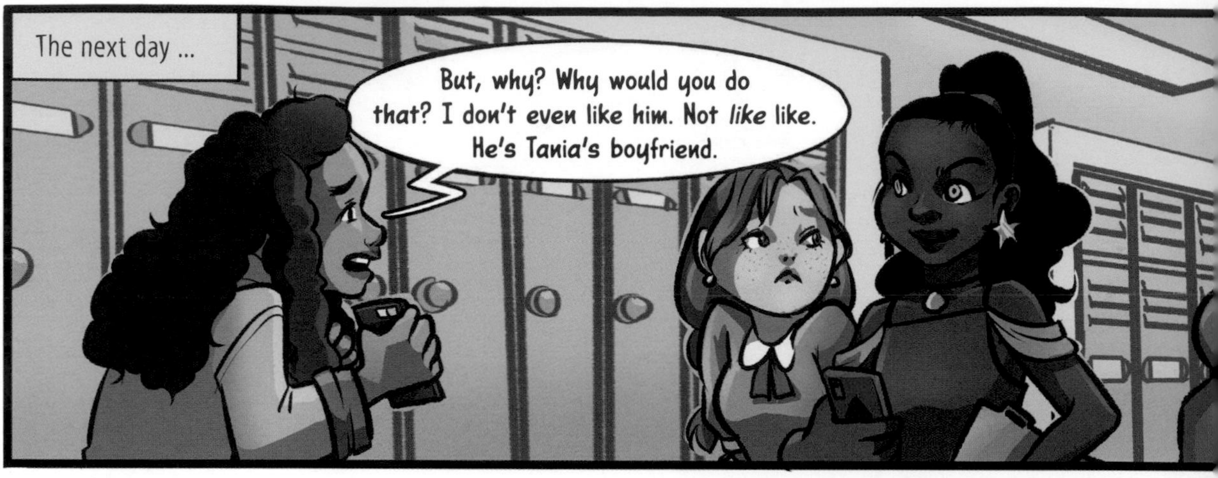
The next day ...
But, why? Why would you do that? I don't even like him. Not *like* like. He's Tania's boyfriend.

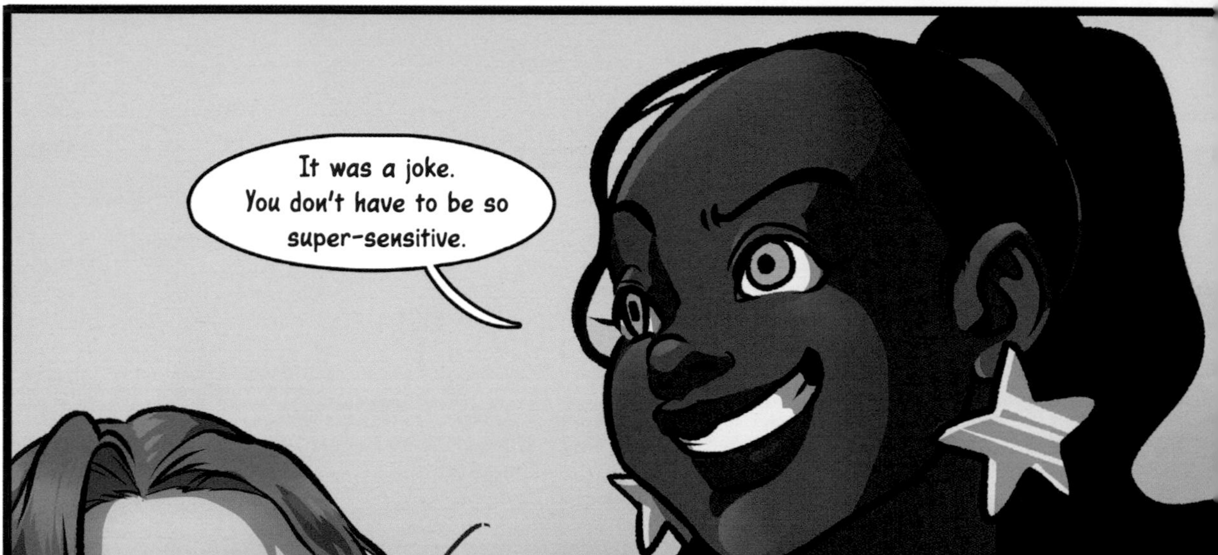
It was a joke. You don't have to be so super-sensitive.

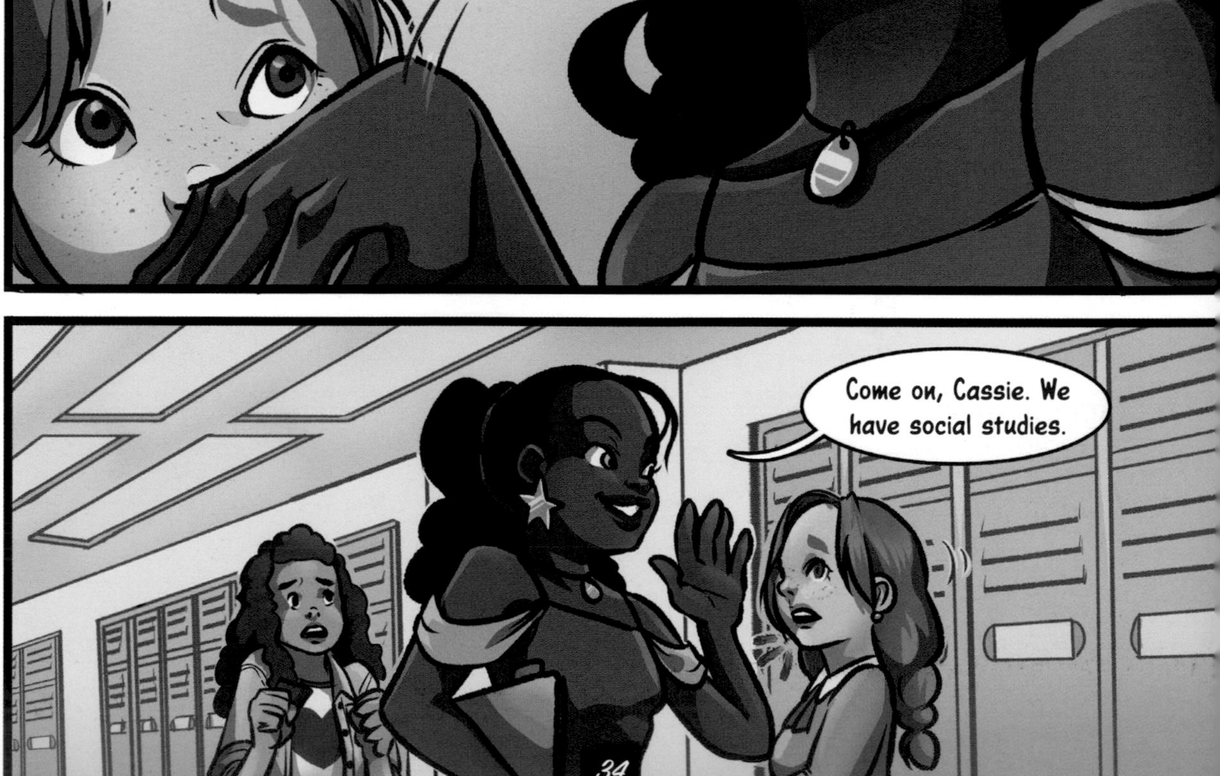
Come on, Cassie. We have social studies.

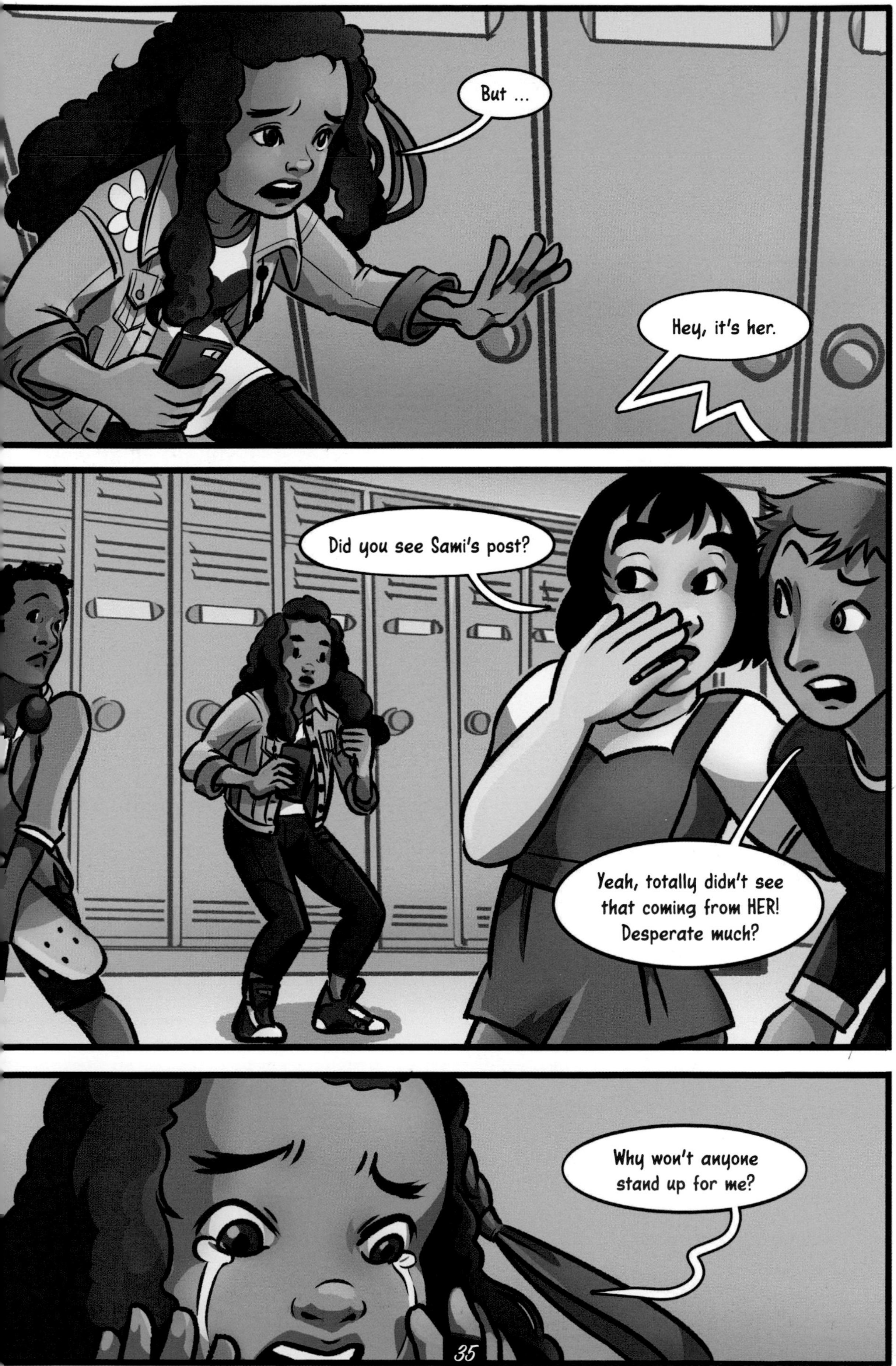
But ...
Hey, it's her.
Did you see Sami's post?
Yeah, totally didn't see that coming from HER! Desperate much?
Why won't anyone stand up for me?

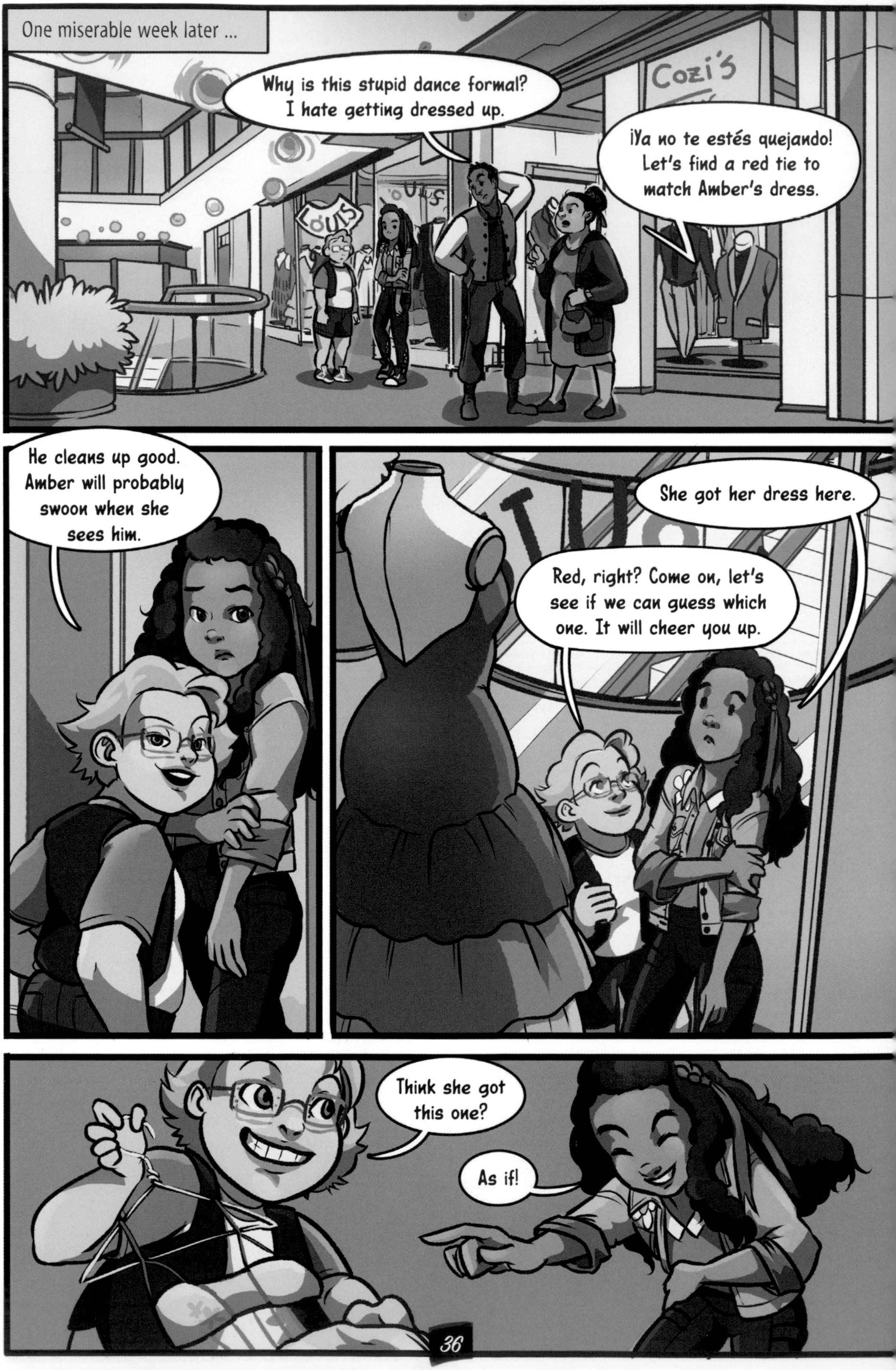
One miserable week later ...
Why is this stupid dance formal? I hate getting dressed up.
COZI'S
LOUIS
¡Ya no te estés quejando! Let's find a red tie to match Amber's dress.
He cleans up good. Amber will probably swoon when she sees him.
She got her dress here.
Red, right? Come on, let's see if we can guess which one. It will cheer you up.
Think she got this one?
As if!

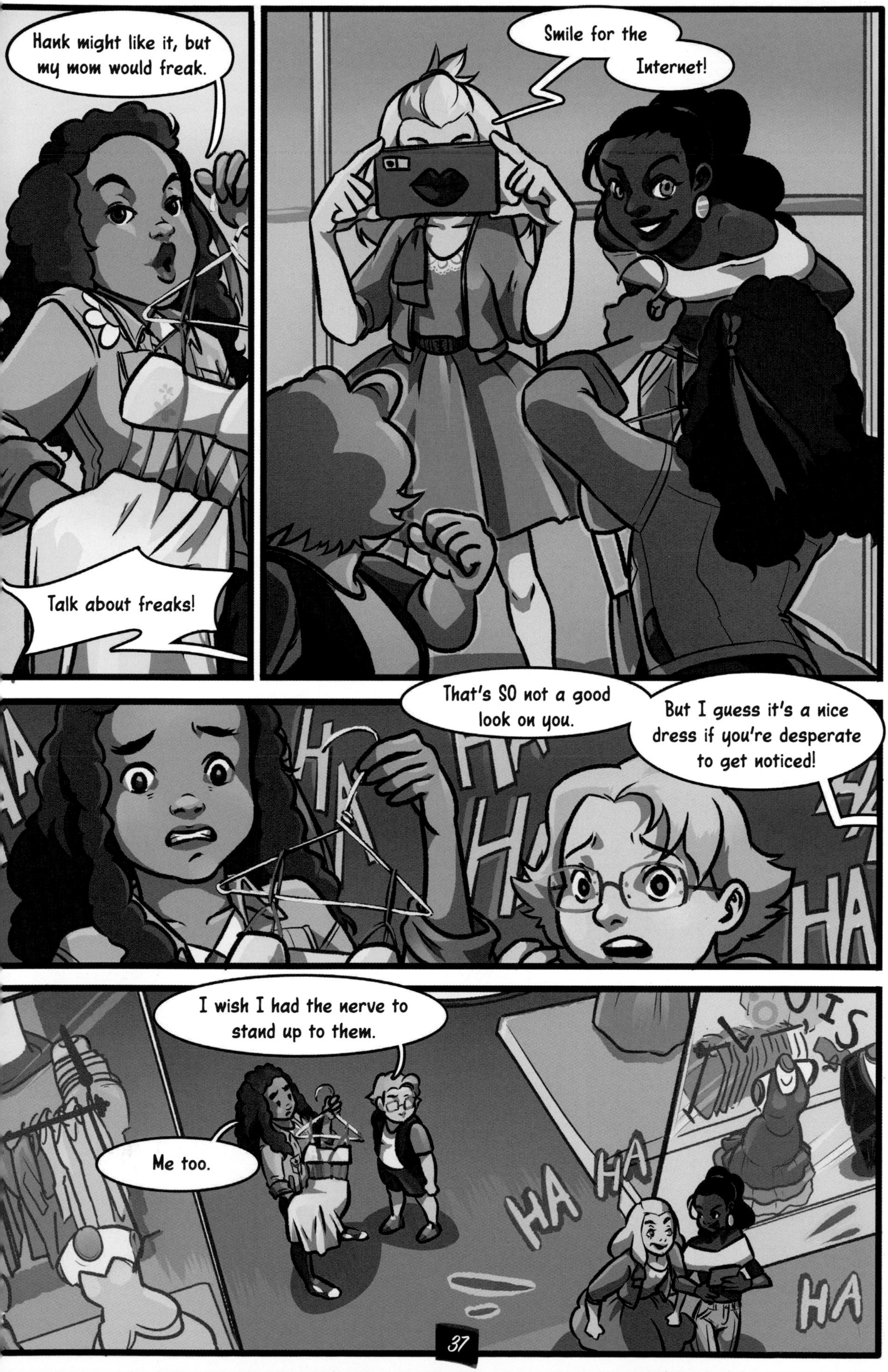

Hank might like it, but my mom would freak.
Talk about freaks!
Smile for the Internet!
That's SO not a good look on you.
But I guess it's a nice dress if you're desperate to get noticed!
HA
I wish I had the nerve to stand up to them.
Me too.
HA
HA
HA

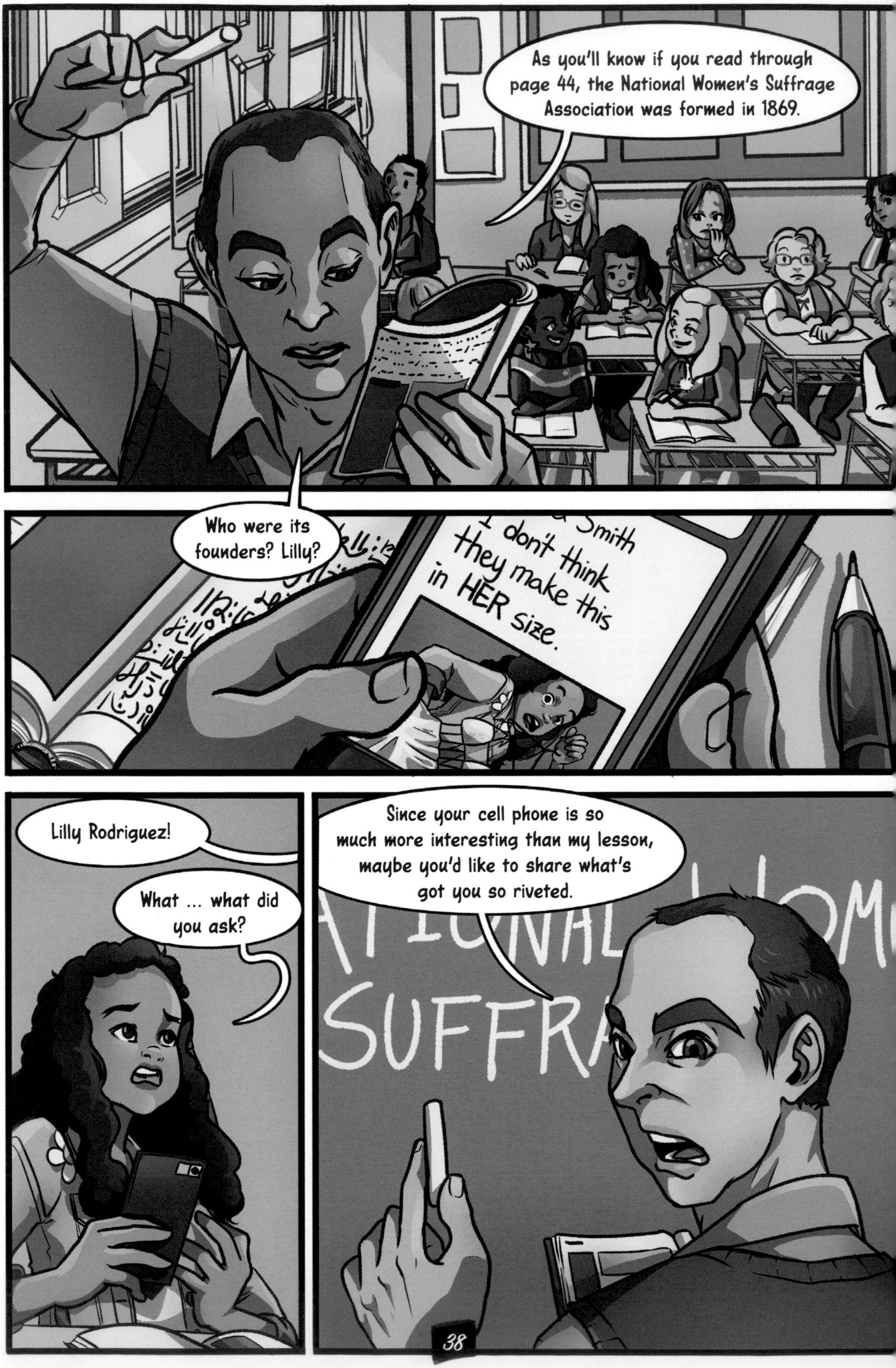
As you'll know if you read through page 44, the National Women's Suffrage Association was formed in 1869.
Who were its founders? Lilly?
I don't think they make this in HER size.
Lilly Rodriguez!
What ... what did you ask?
Since your cell phone is so much more interesting than my lesson, maybe you'd like to share what's got you so riveted.
SUFFRA

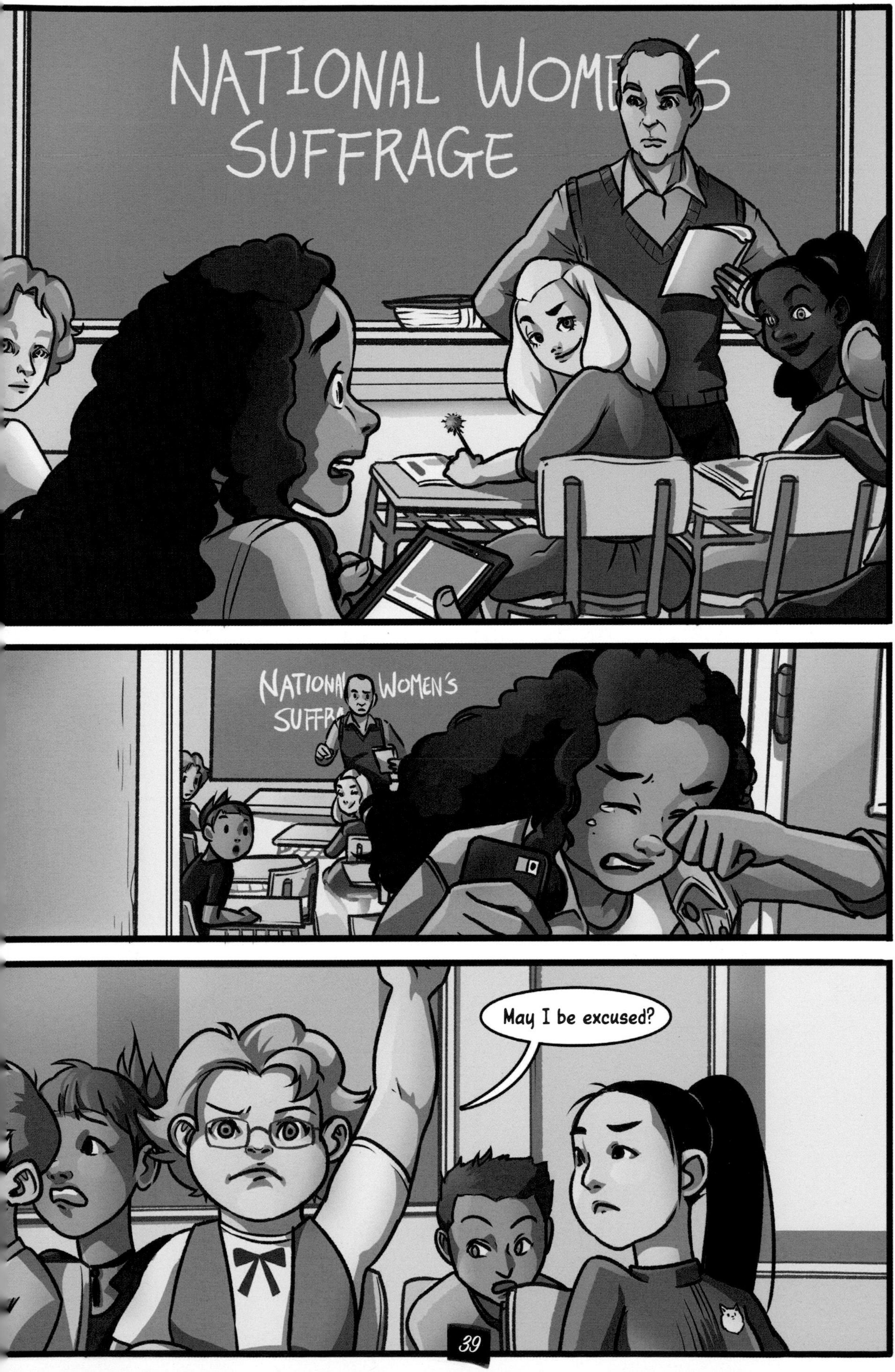
NATIONAL
SUFFRAGE
WOMEN'S
May I be excused?

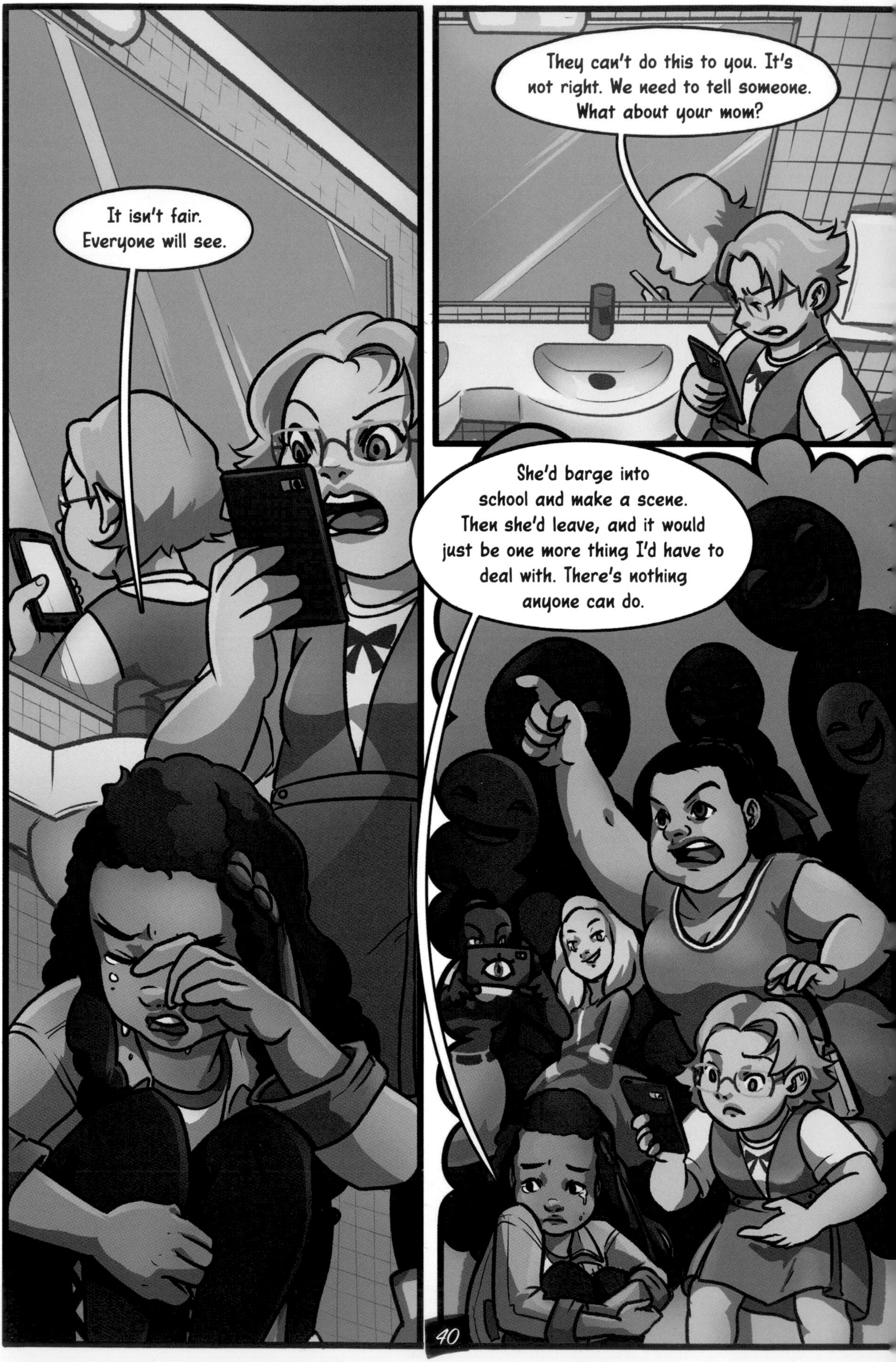
It isn't fair. Everyone will see.
They can't do this to you. It's not right. We need to tell someone. What about your mom?
She'd barge into school and make a scene. Then she'd leave, and it would just be one more thing I'd have to deal with. There's nothing anyone can do.

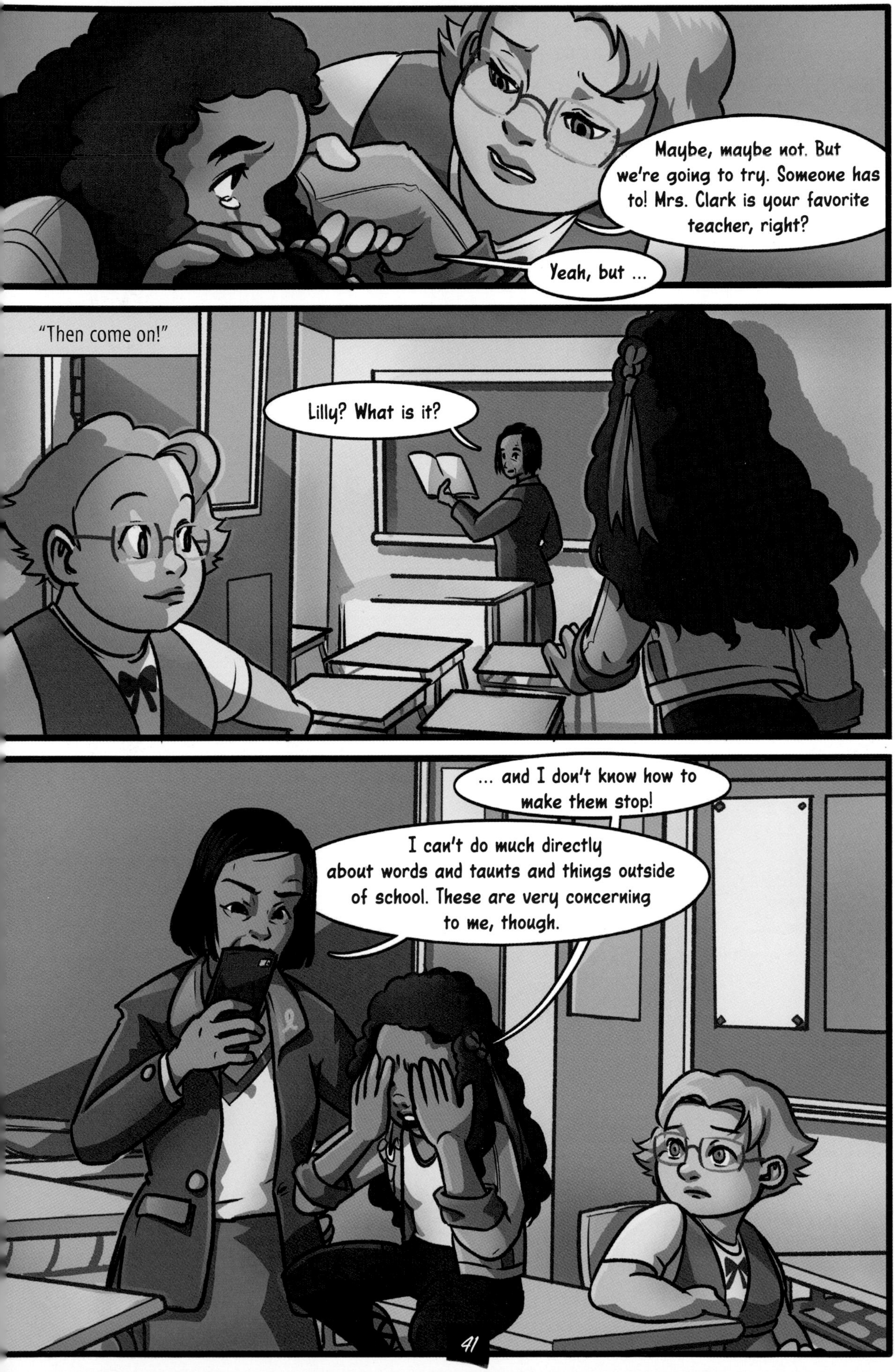
Maybe, maybe not. But we're going to try. Someone has to! Mrs. Clark is your favorite teacher, right?
Yeah, but ...
"Then come on!"
Lilly? What is it?
... and I don't know how to make them stop!
I can't do much directly about words and taunts and things outside of school. These are very concerning to me, though.

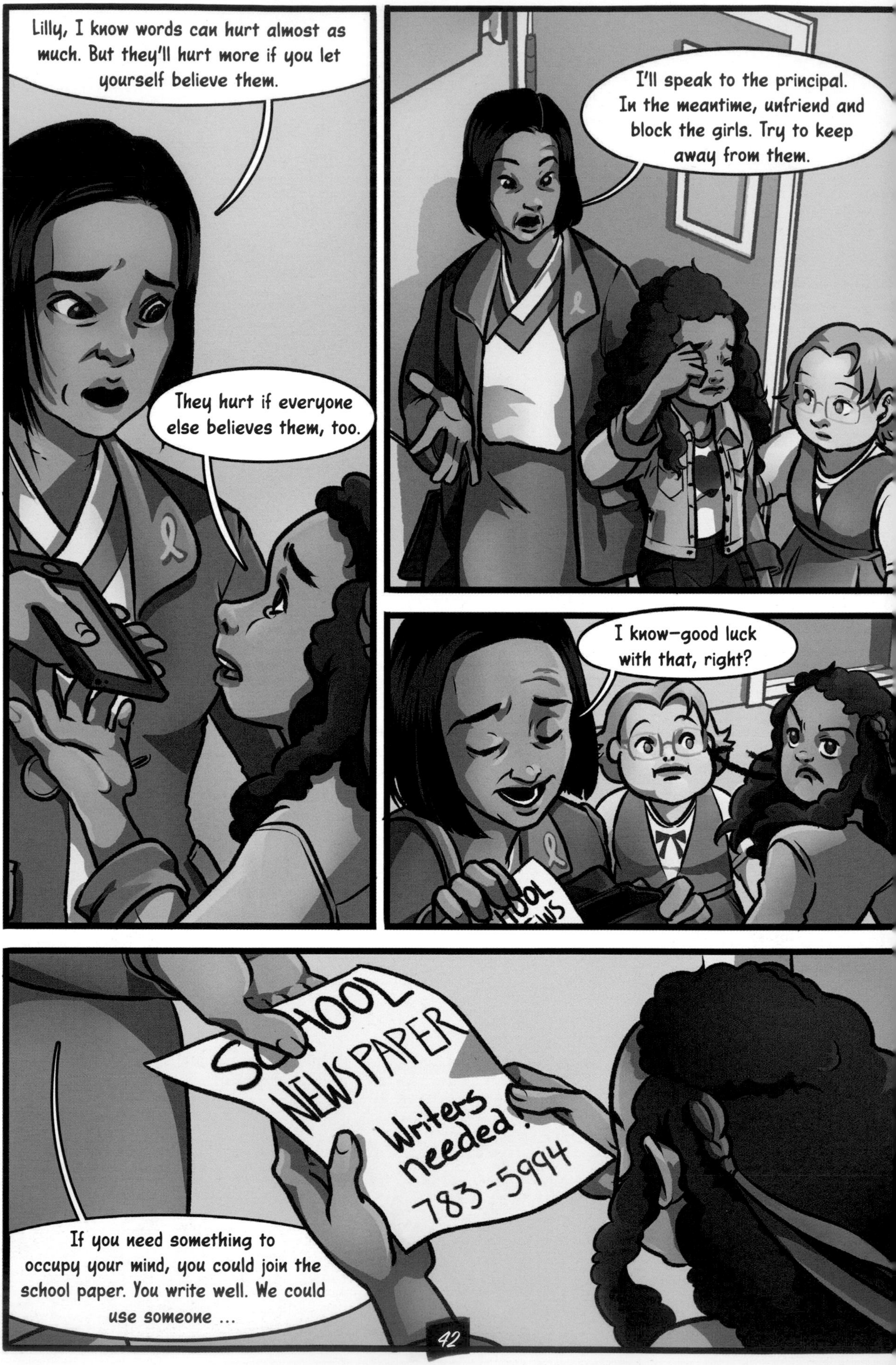
Lilly, I know words can hurt almost as much. But they'll hurt more if you let yourself believe them.
They hurt if everyone else believes them, too.
I'll speak to the principal. In the meantime, unfriend and block the girls. Try to keep away from them.
I know—good luck with that, right?
SCHOOL NEWSPAPER
Writers needed!
783-5994
If you need something to occupy your mind, you could join the school paper. You write well. We could use someone ...

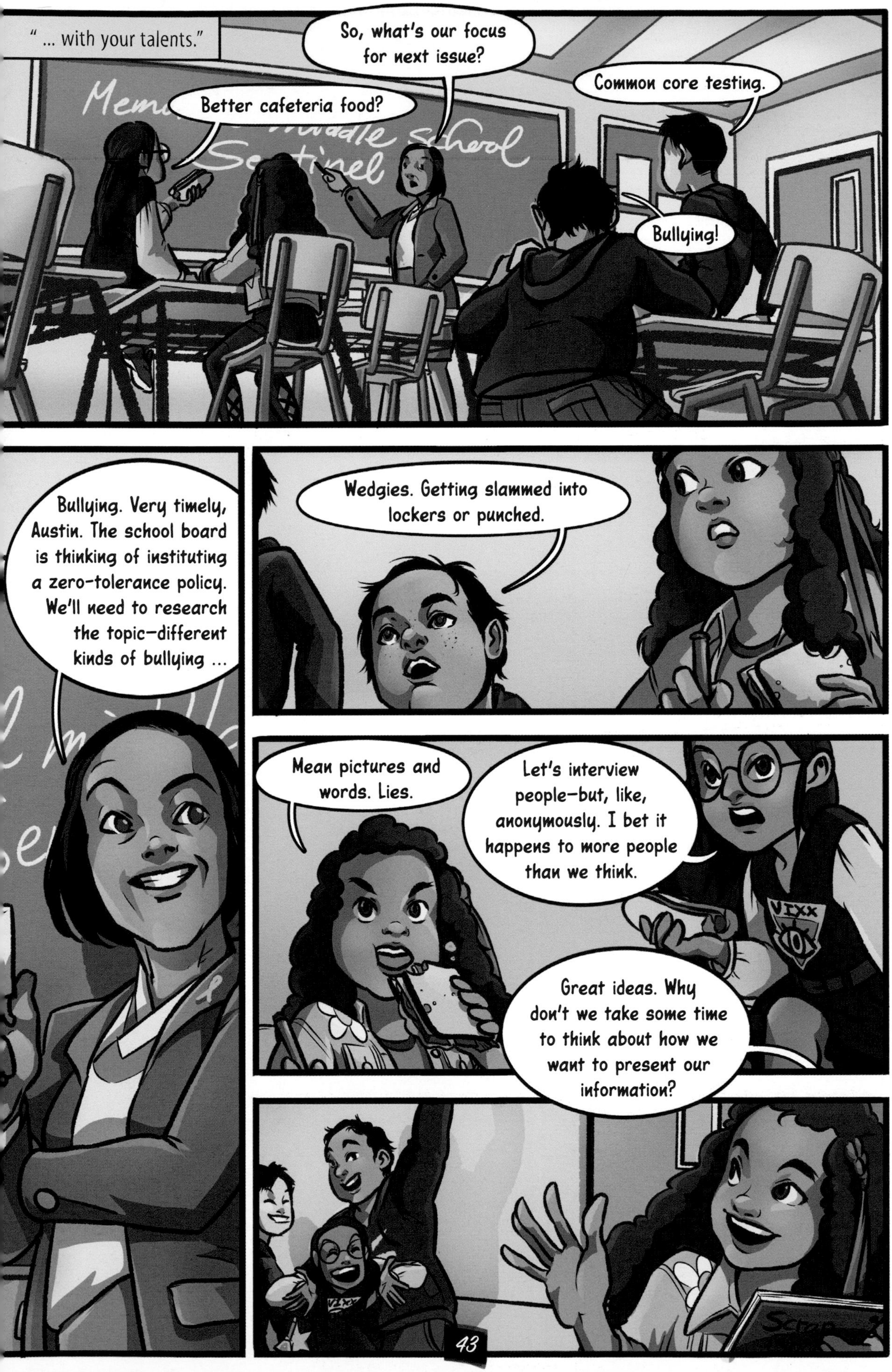
" ... with your talents."
So, what's our focus for next issue?
Better cafeteria food?
Common core testing.
Bullying!
Bullying. Very timely, Austin. The school board is thinking of instituting a zero-tolerance policy. We'll need to research the topic—different kinds of bullying ...
Wedgies. Getting slammed into lockers or punched.
Mean pictures and words. Lies.
Let's interview people—but, like, anonymously. I bet it happens to more people than we think.
Great ideas. Why don't we take some time to think about how we want to present our information?

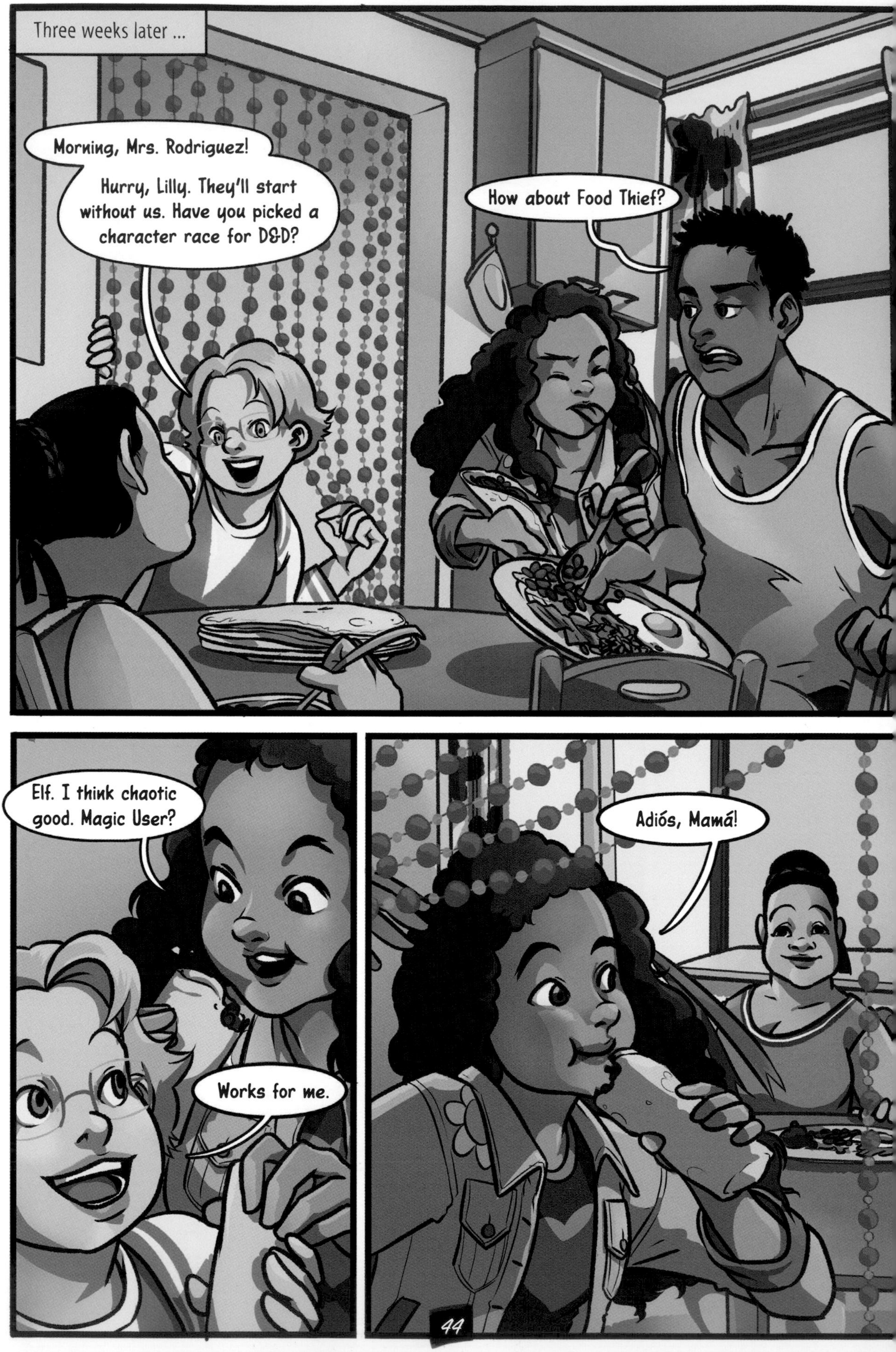
Three weeks later ...
Morning, Mrs. Rodriguez!
Hurry, Lilly. They'll start without us. Have you picked a character race for D&D?
How about Food Thief?
Elf. I think chaotic good. Magic User?
Works for me.
Adiós, Mamá!

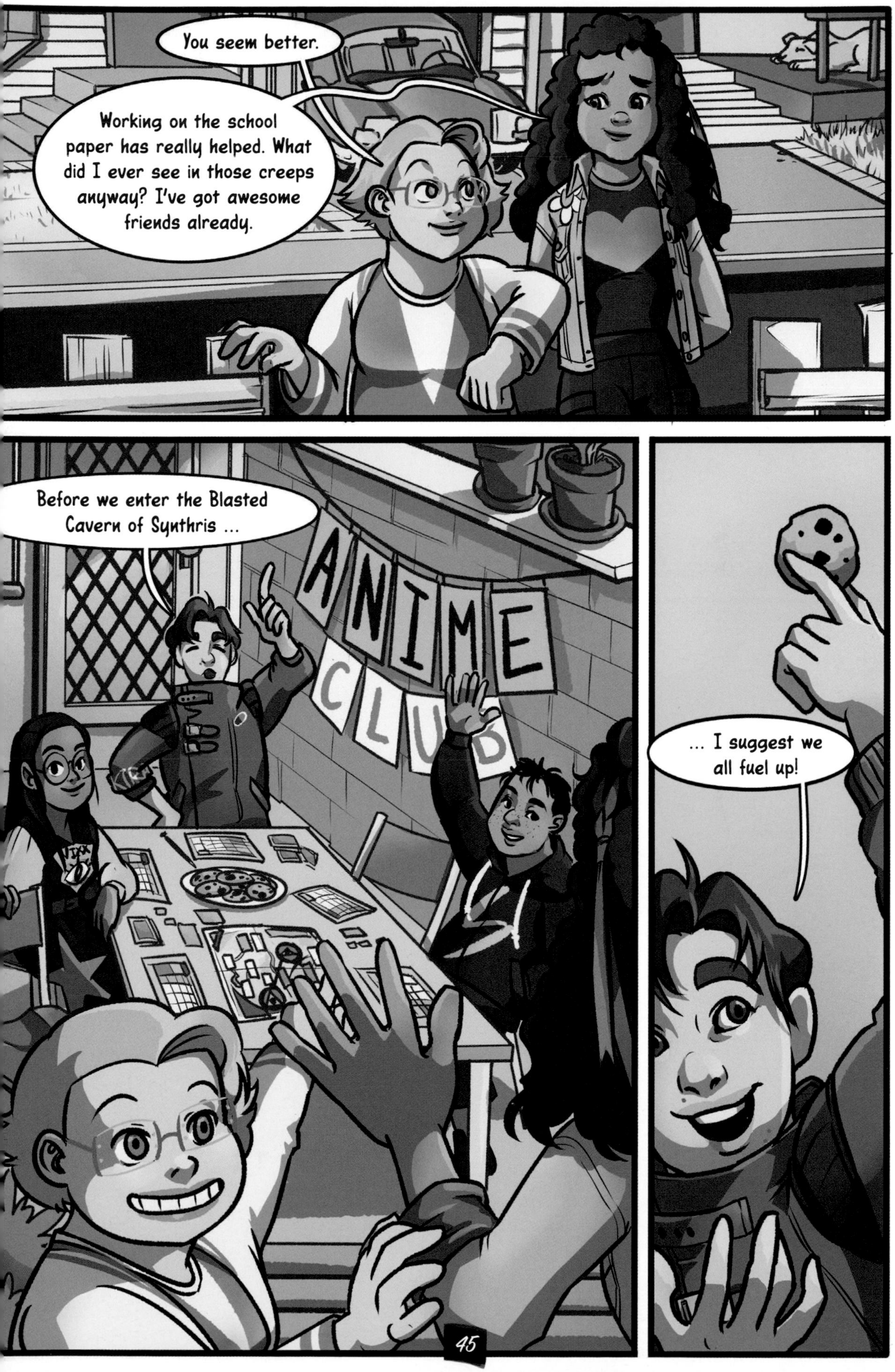
You seem better.
Working on the school paper has really helped. What did I ever see in those creeps anyway? I've got awesome friends already.
Before we enter the Blasted Cavern of Synthris ...
ANIME CLUB
... I suggest we all fuel up!

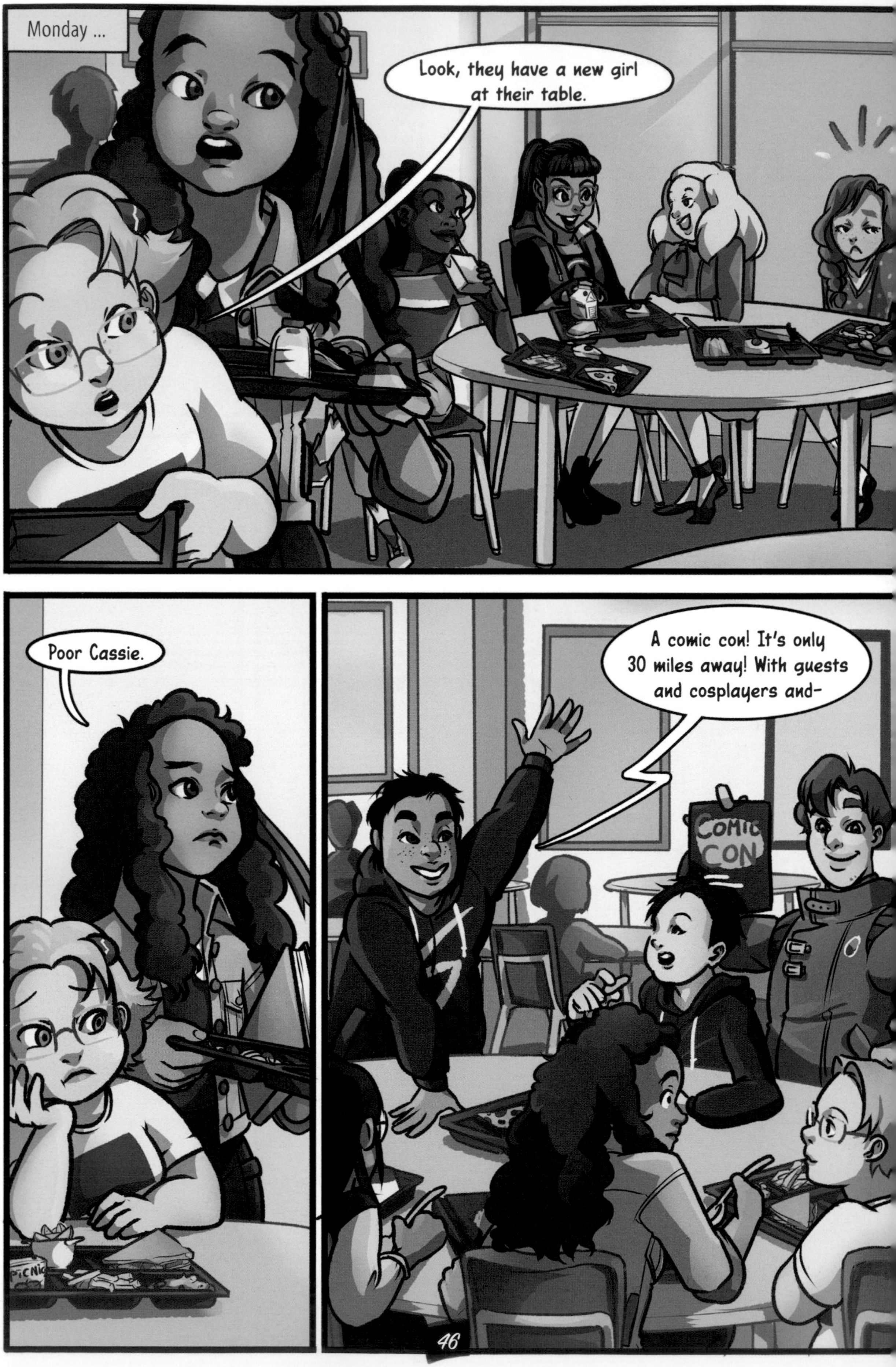
Monday ...
Look, they have a new girl at their table.
Poor Cassie.
A comic con! It's only 30 miles away! With guests and cosplayers and-
COMIC CON

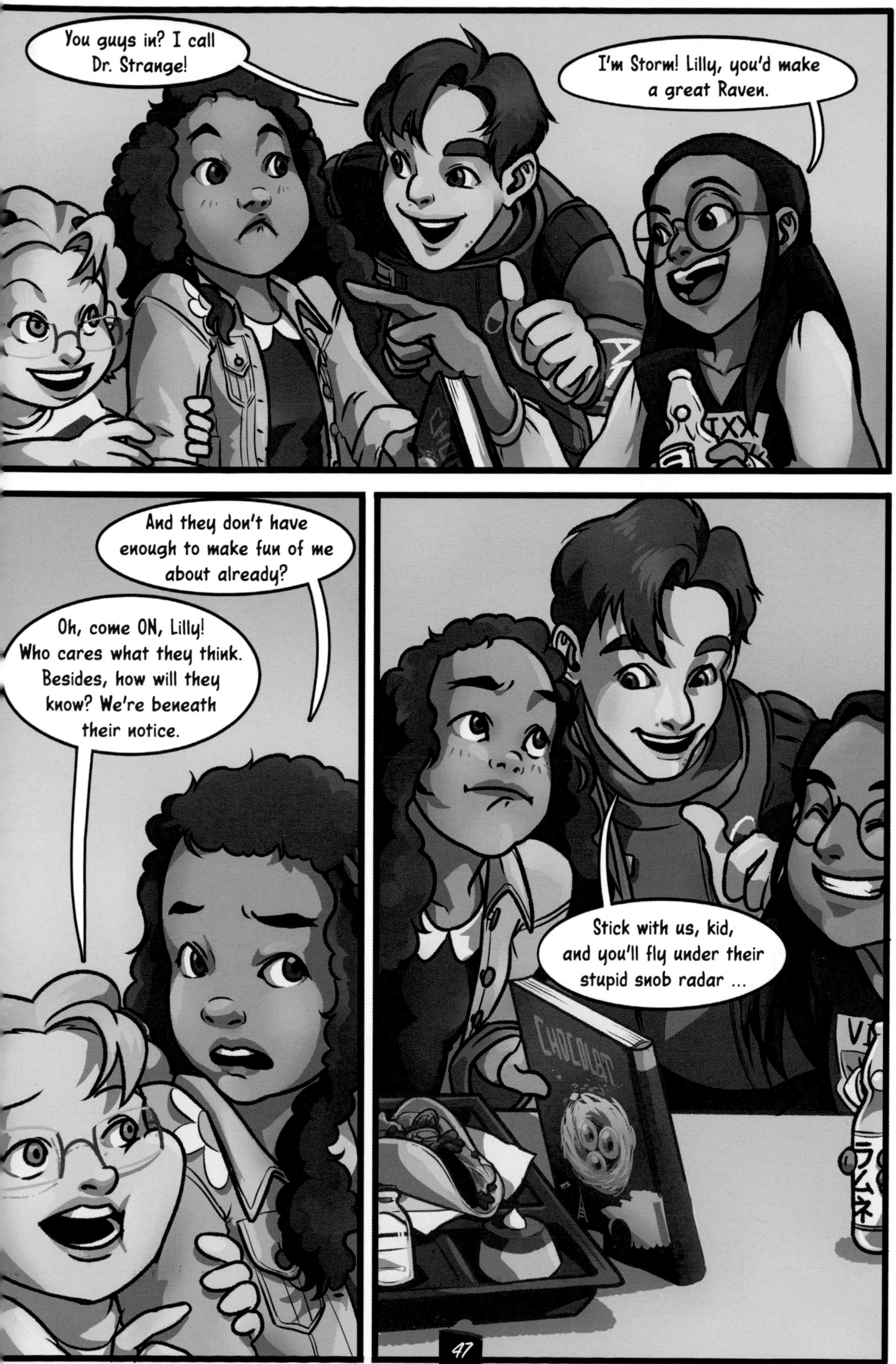
You guys in? I call Dr. Strange!
I'm Storm! Lilly, you'd make a great Raven.
And they don't have enough to make fun of me about already?
Oh, come ON, Lilly! Who cares what they think. Besides, how will they know? We're beneath their notice.
Stick with us, kid, and you'll fly under their stupid snob radar ...

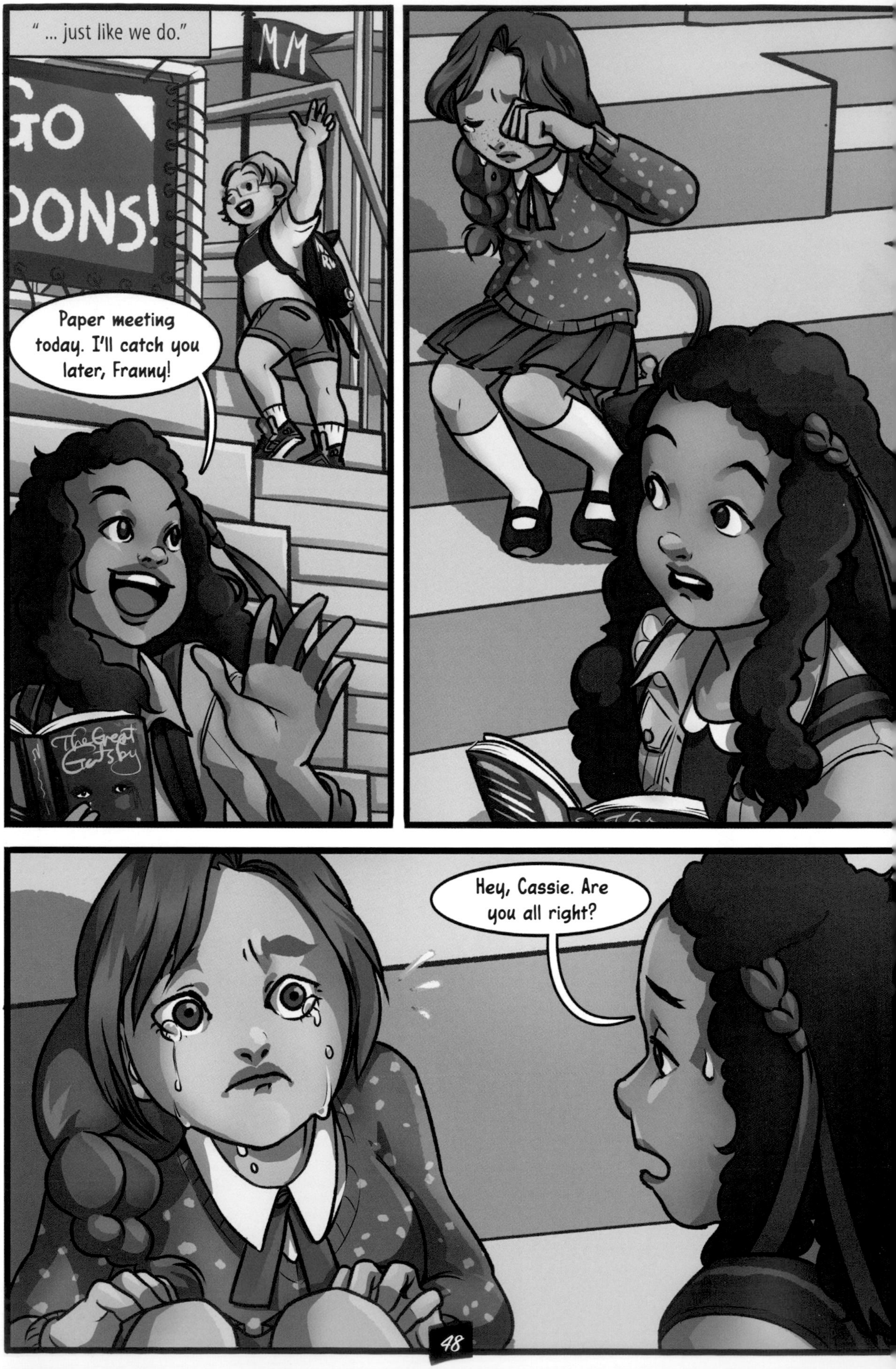
" ... just like we do."
Paper meeting today. I'll catch you later, Franny!
The Great Gatsby
Hey, Cassie. Are you all right?

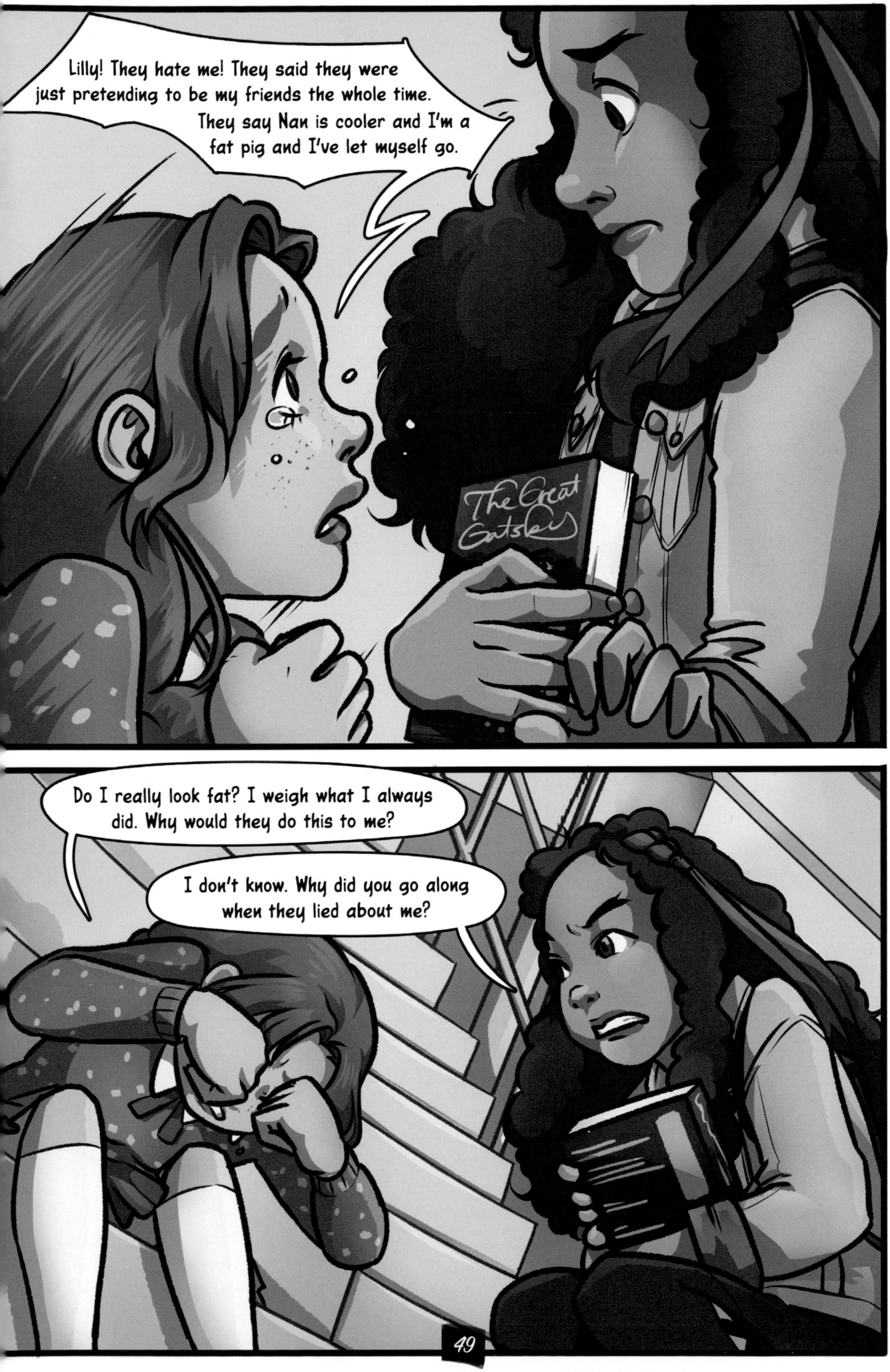
Lilly! They hate me! They said they were just pretending to be my friends the whole time.
They say Nan is cooler and I'm a fat pig and I've let myself go.
The Great Gatsby
Do I really look fat? I weigh what I always did. Why would they do this to me?
I don't know. Why did you go along when they lied about me?

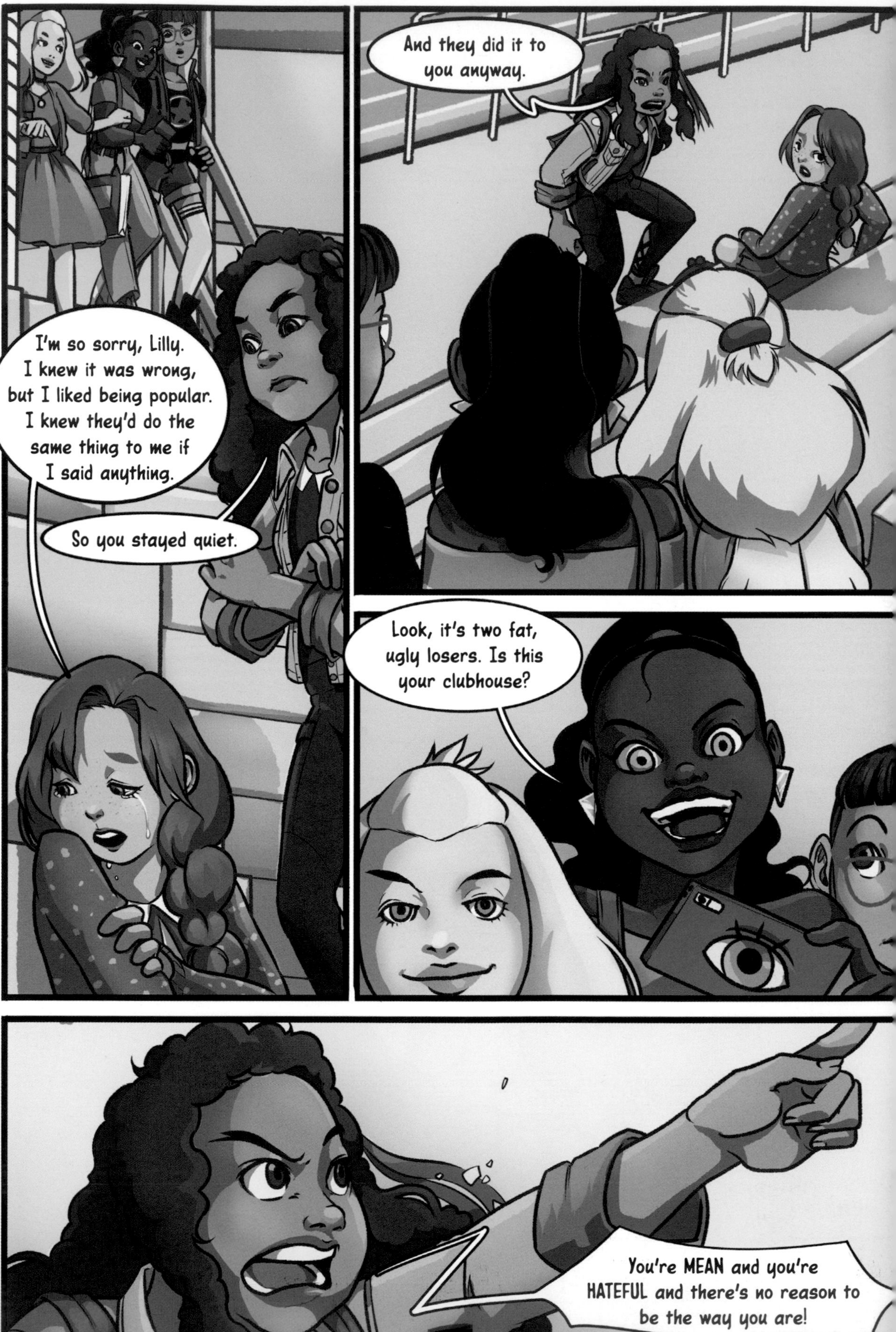
I'm so sorry, Lilly. I knew it was wrong, but I liked being popular. I knew they'd do the same thing to me if I said anything.
So you stayed quiet.
And they did it to you anyway.
Look, it's two fat, ugly losers. Is this your clubhouse?
You're MEAN and you're HATEFUL and there's no reason to be the way you are!

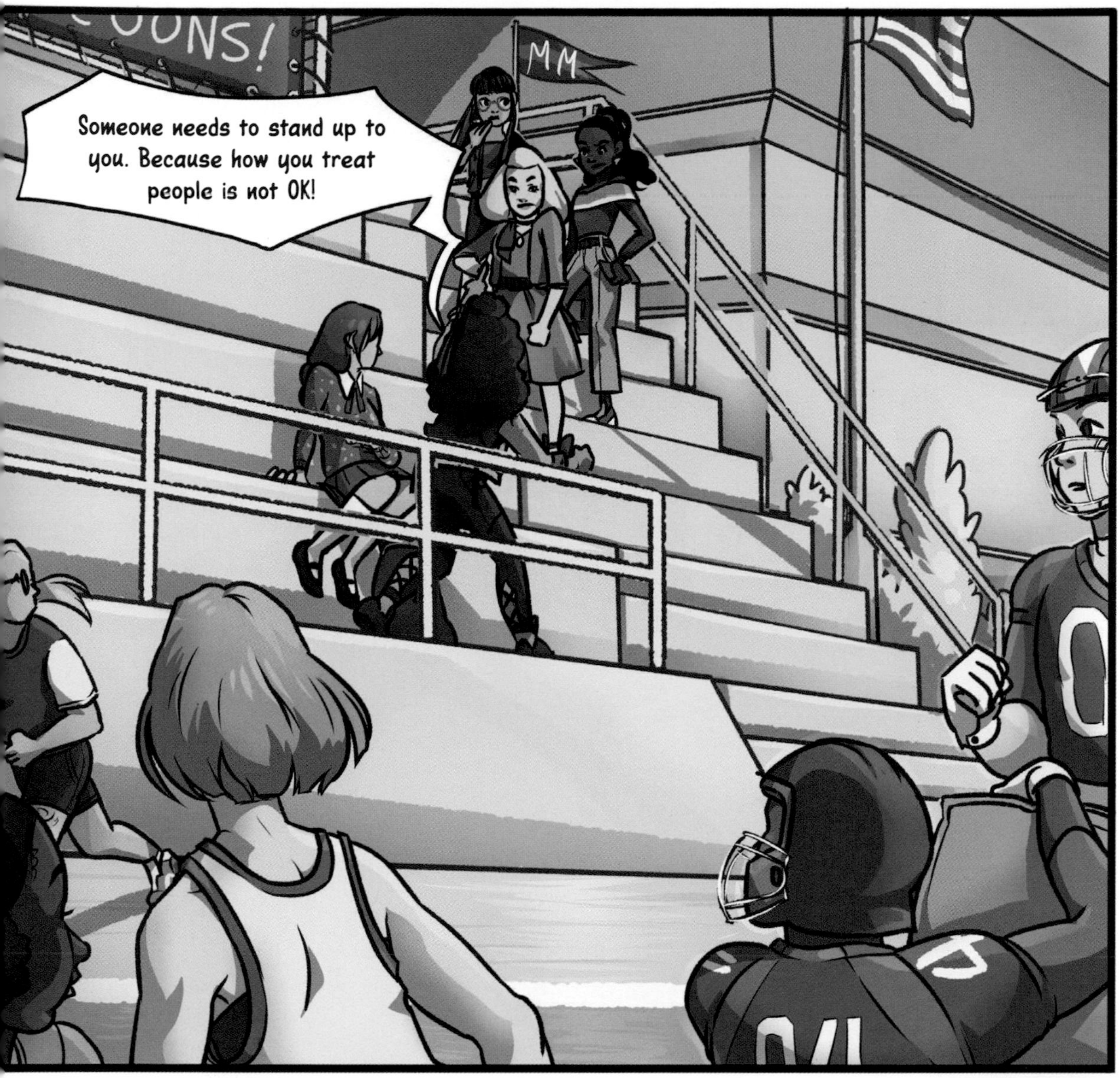
MM
Someone needs to stand up to you. Because how you treat people is not OK!

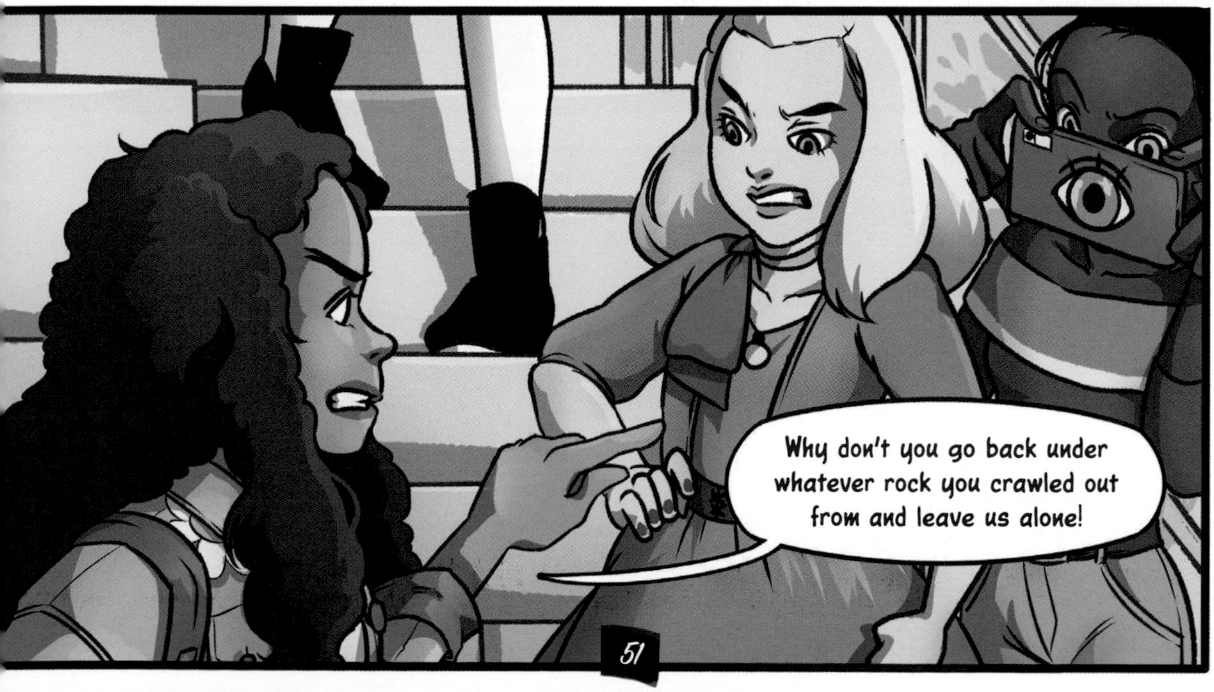
Why don't you go back under whatever rock you crawled out from and leave us alone!

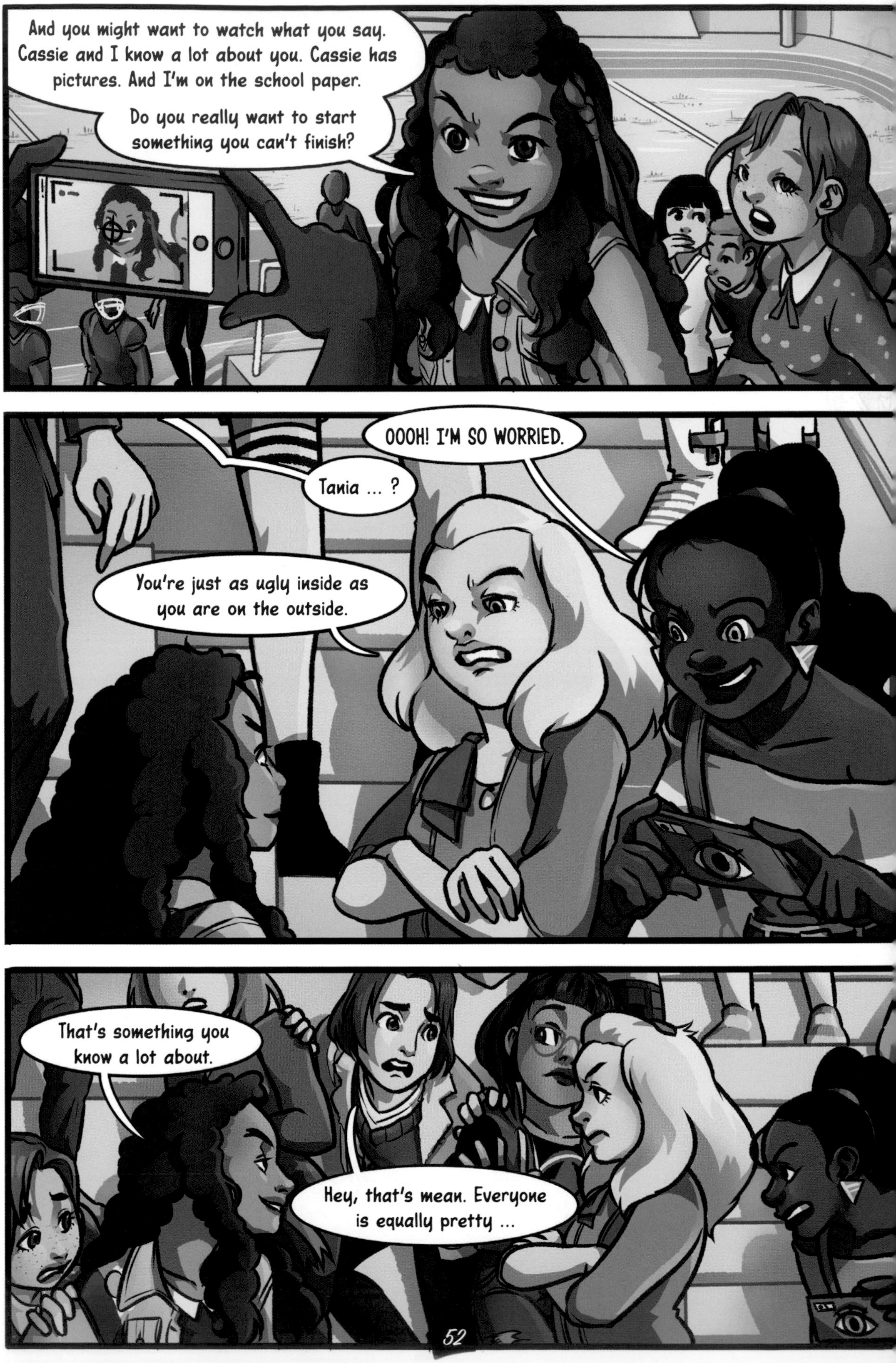

And you might want to watch what you say. Cassie and I know a lot about you. Cassie has pictures. And I'm on the school paper.
Do you really want to start something you can't finish?
OOOH! I'M SO WORRIED.
Tania ... ?
You're just as ugly inside as you are on the outside.
That's something you know a lot about.
Hey, that's mean. Everyone is equally pretty ...

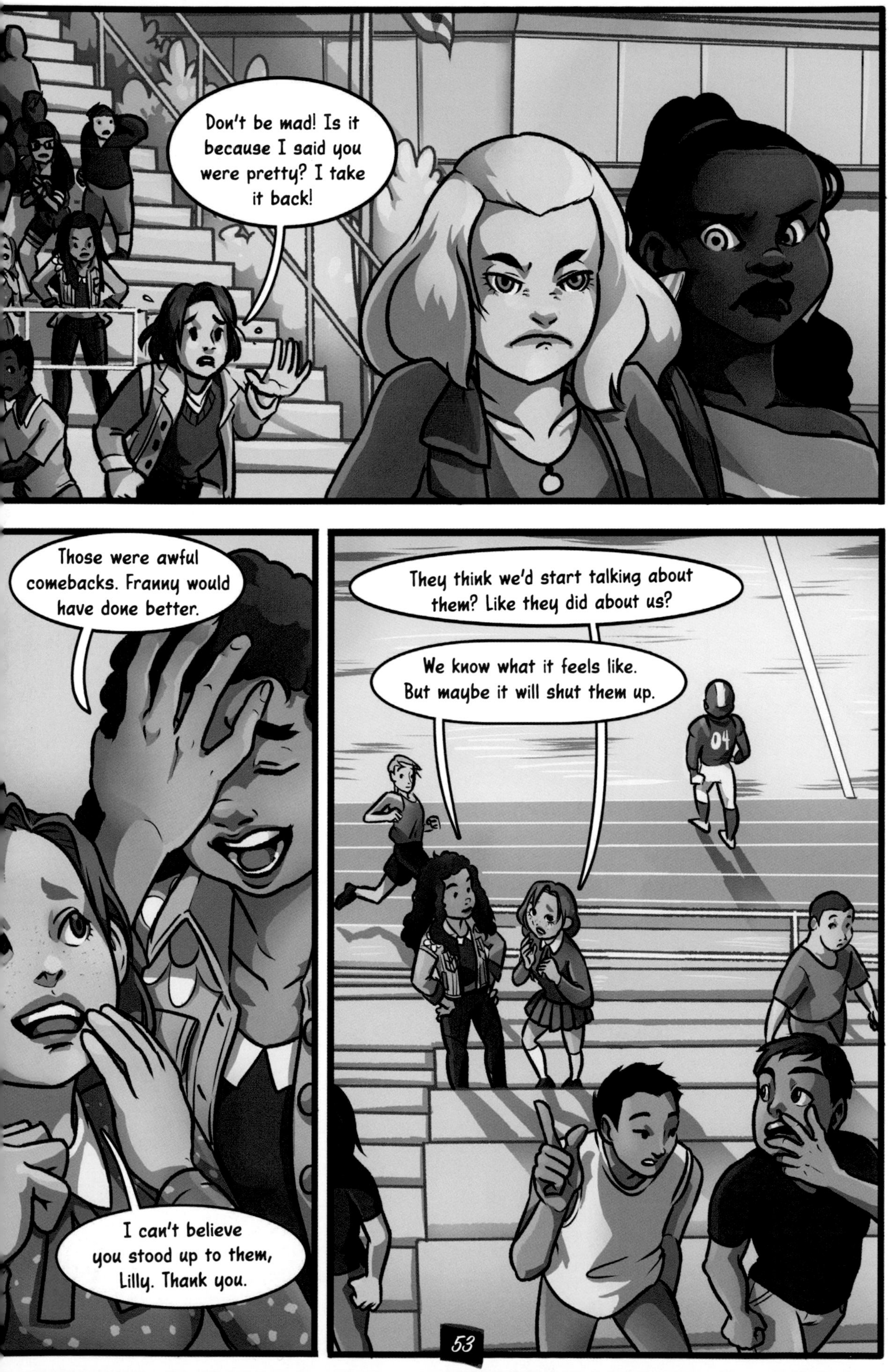
Don't be mad! Is it because I said you were pretty? I take it back!
Those were awful comebacks. Franny would have done better.
I can't believe you stood up to them, Lilly. Thank you.
They think we'd start talking about them? Like they did about us?
We know what it feels like. But maybe it will shut them up.
04

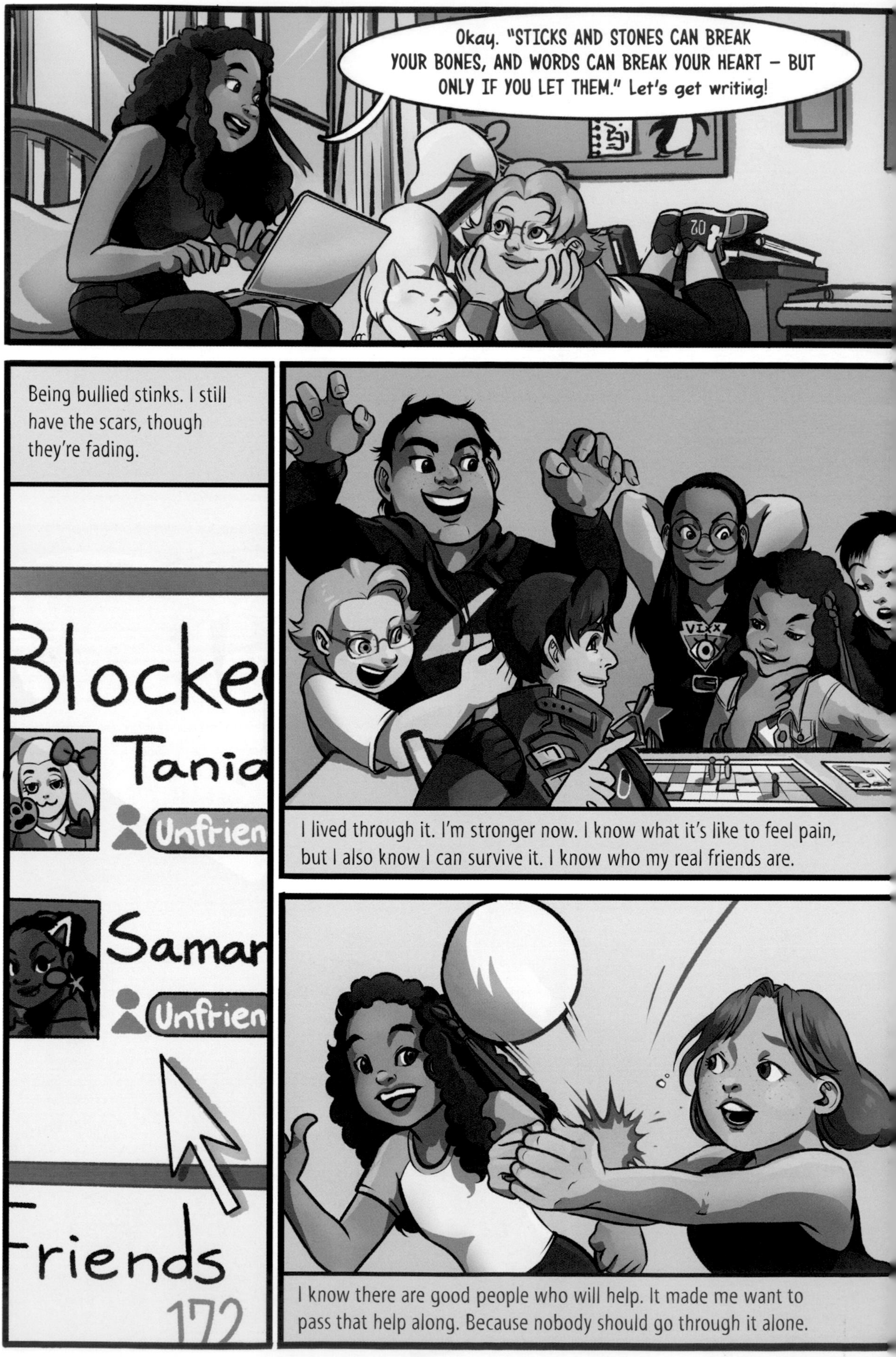
Okay. "STICKS AND STONES CAN BREAK YOUR BONES, AND WORDS CAN BREAK YOUR HEART – BUT ONLY IF YOU LET THEM." Let's get writing!
Being bullied stinks. I still have the scars, though they're fading.
Blocke
Tania
Unfrien
Samar
Unfrien
Friends
VIXX
I lived through it. I'm stronger now. I know what it's like to feel pain, but I also know I can survive it. I know who my real friends are.
I know there are good people who will help. It made me want to pass that help along. Because nobody should go through it alone.

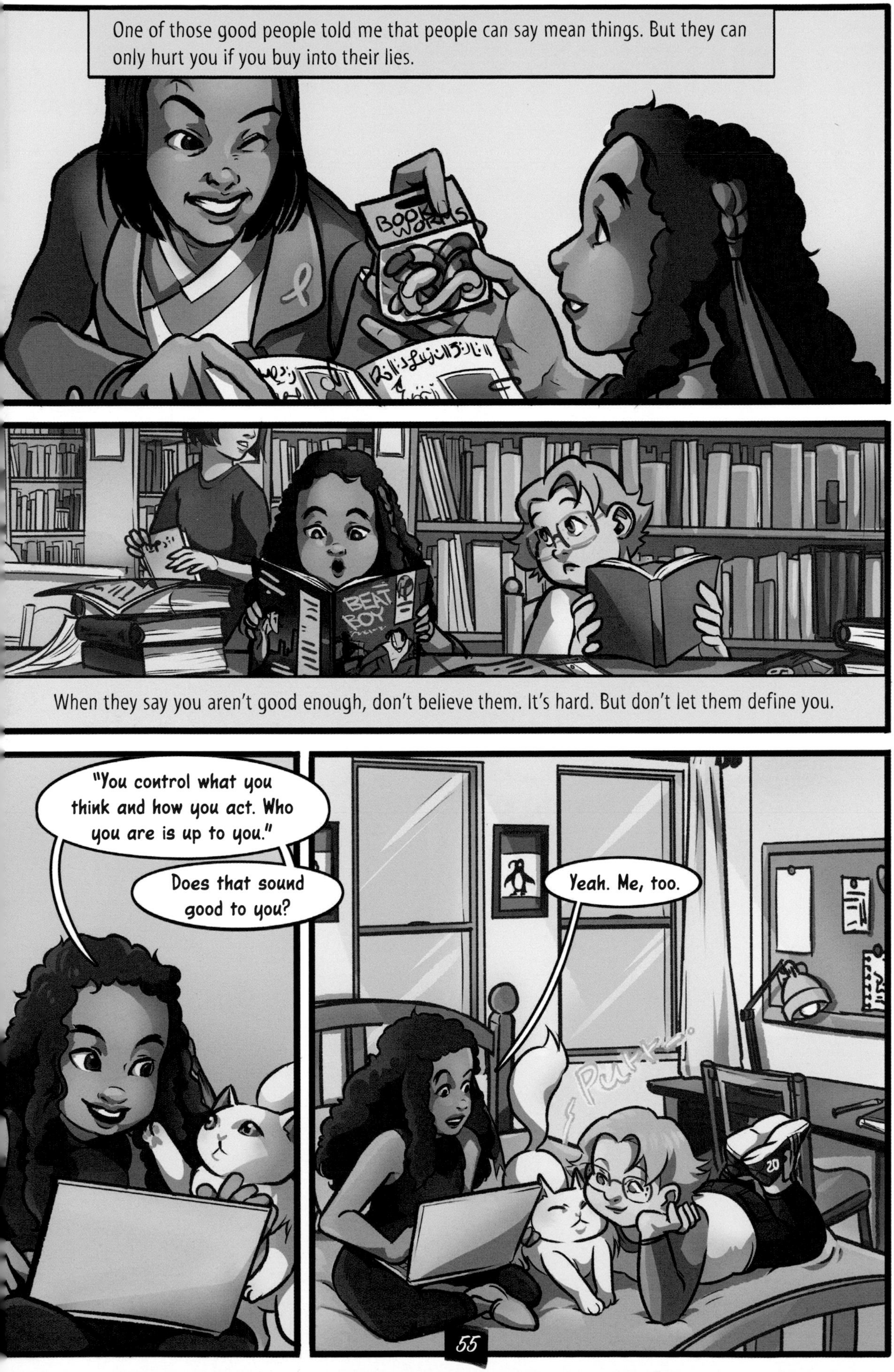
One of those good people told me that people can say mean things. But they can only hurt you if you buy into their lies.
BOOKWORMS
BEAT BOY
When they say you aren't good enough, don't believe them. It's hard. But don't let them define you.
"You control what you think and how you act. Who you are is up to you."
Does that sound good to you?
Yeah. Me, too.

# School Newspaper Team

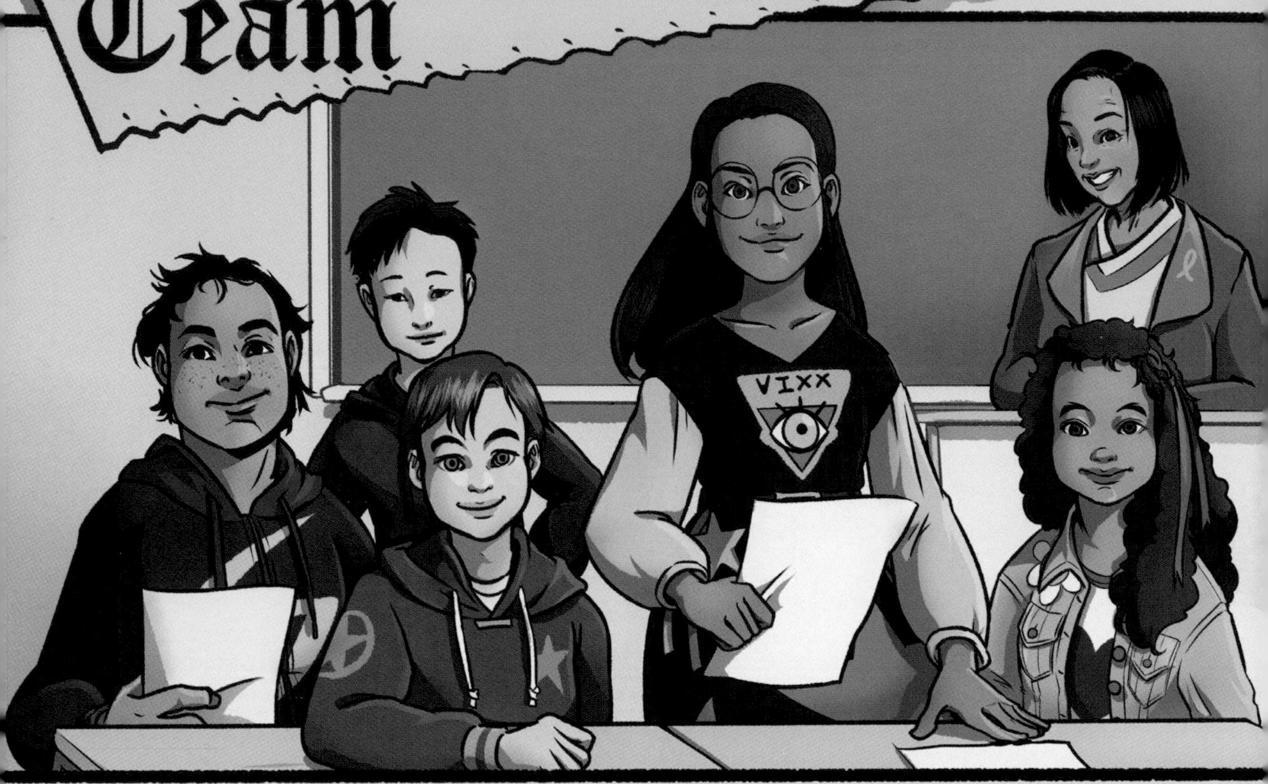
VIXX

The truth is out there! Our newspaper team (from left to right: Austin Cooper, David Yu, Tyler Cain, Jenny Book, and Lilly Rodriguez) is on the job, searching for scoops and typing up taglines. Go, Team!

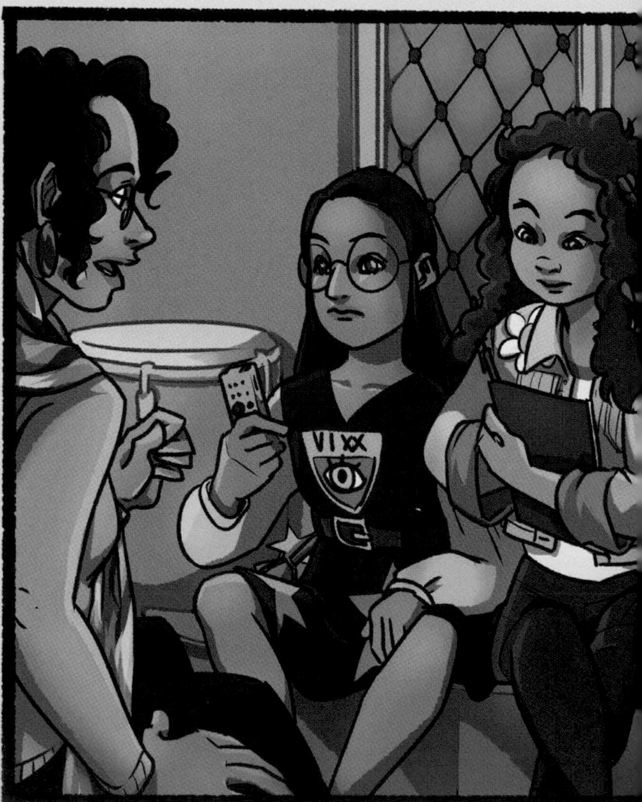
VIXX

The choir teacher, Ms. Gray, gives Jenny and Lilly the scoop on the upcoming musical, KATS. She wrote it herself!

A good reporter always checks their facts! There's nowhere like the library.

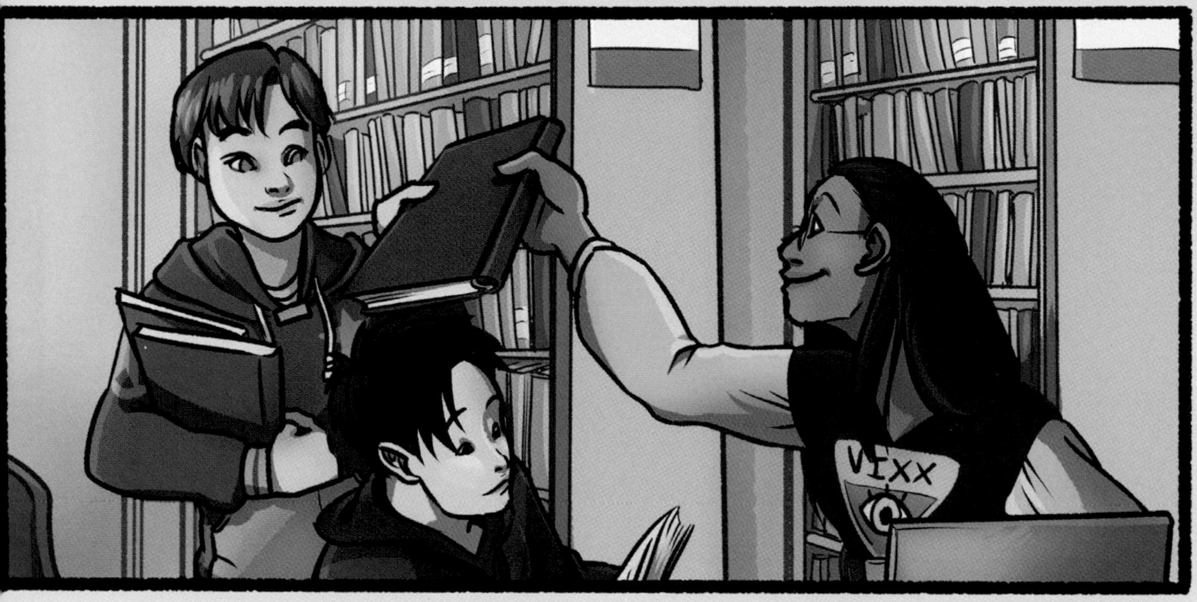
VIXX

Sometimes you just need a little bit of sugar to get through the day.

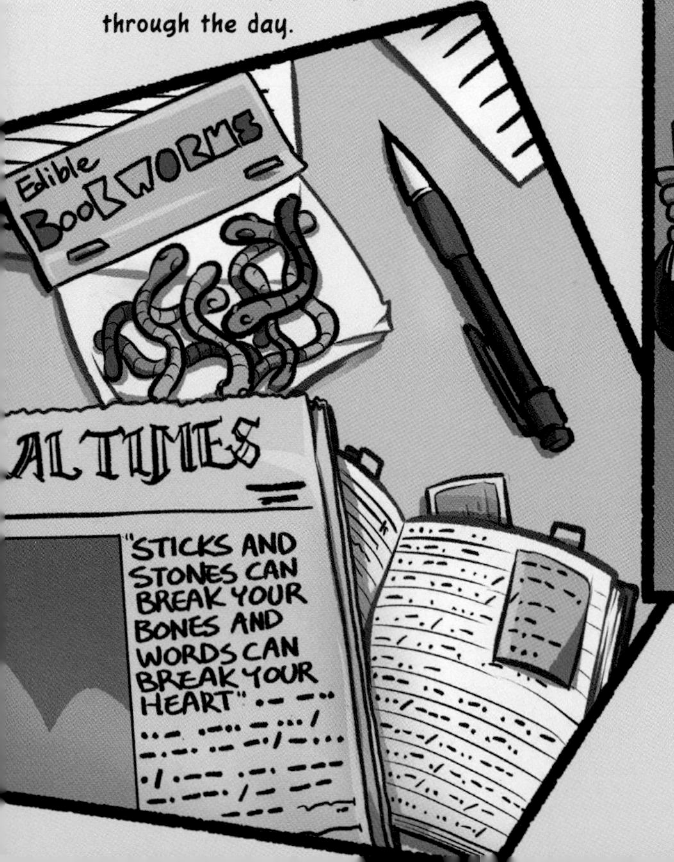
Edible
BooKWORMS
AL TIMES
"STICKS AND STONES CAN BREAK YOUR BONES AND WORDS CAN BREAK YOUR HEART"

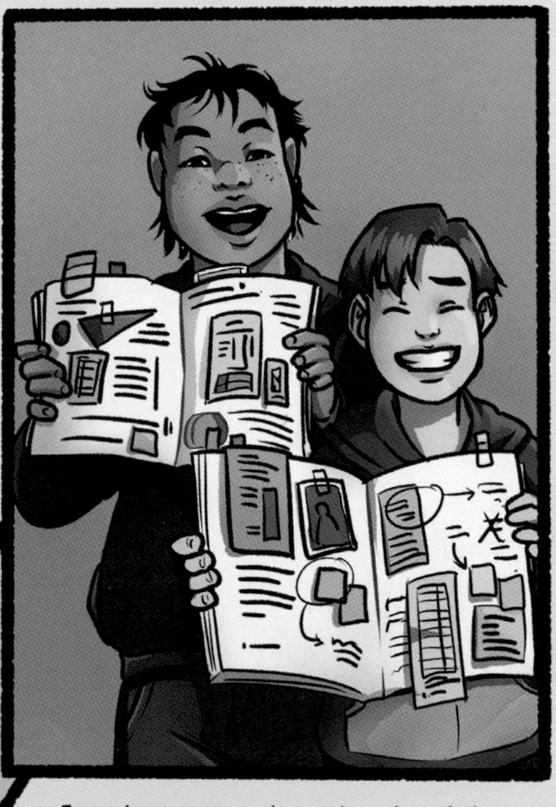

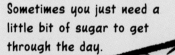

It isn't an easy job to plan the whole paper, but someone has to do it—our layout editors are the best!

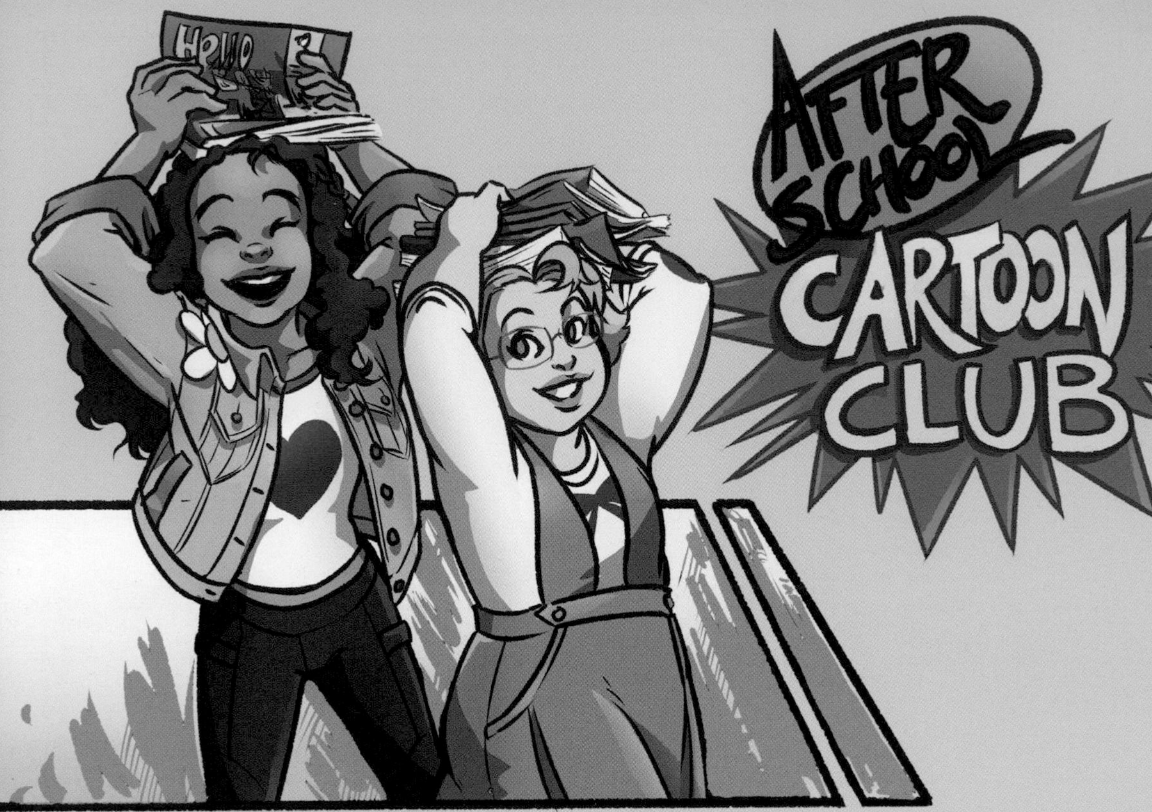
AFTER SCHOOL
CARTOON CLUB

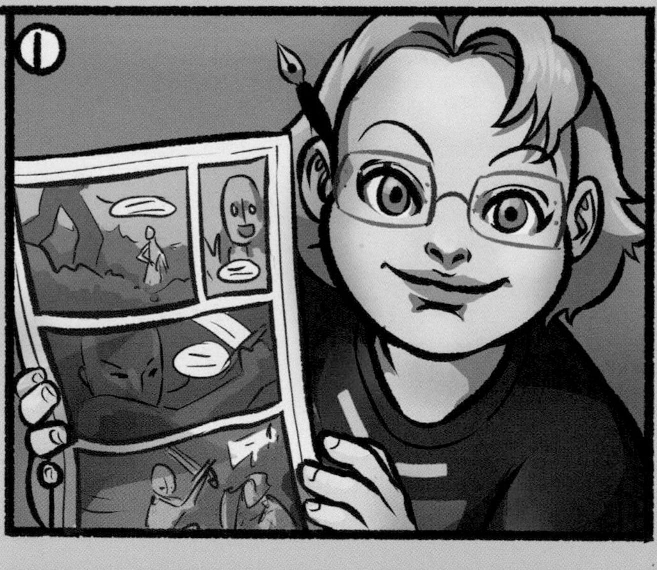

① Founding-member and all-around all star Franny Luca is hoping to be the next big thing in comics. She's conquering the world one panel at a time!

② Franny Luca (left) and Austin Cooper (right) are always reading! It doesn't matter if it's right to left, left to right, up, down, or sideways—if there's a story, they'll pick it up.

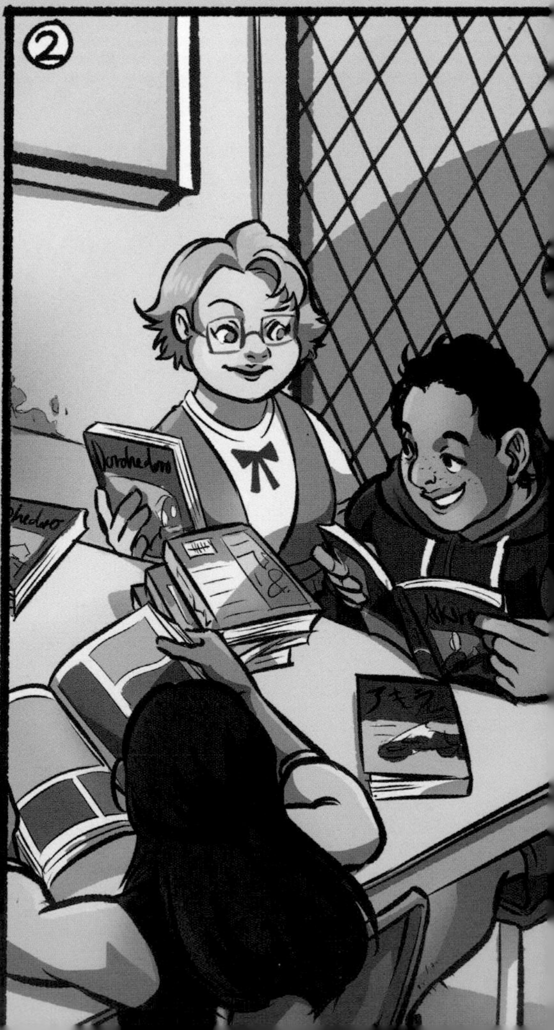

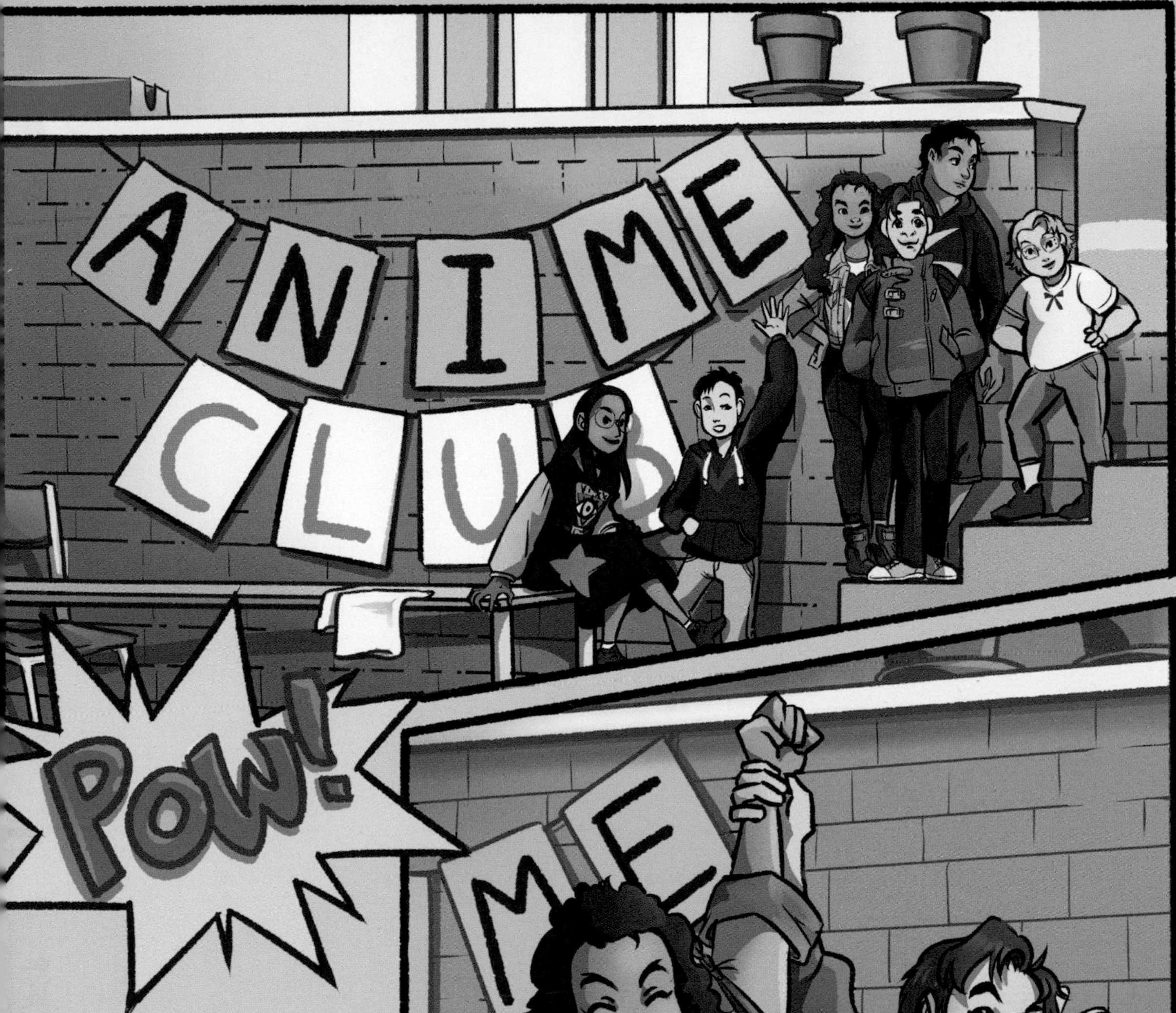
ANIME
CLUB
POW!

We don't just read comics and watch anime. There's also the wide world of tabletop gaming to explore! Flip a card, roll a 10-sided dice, or break out your player's handbook. Dungeon Master Scooter deJesus is always ready to play!

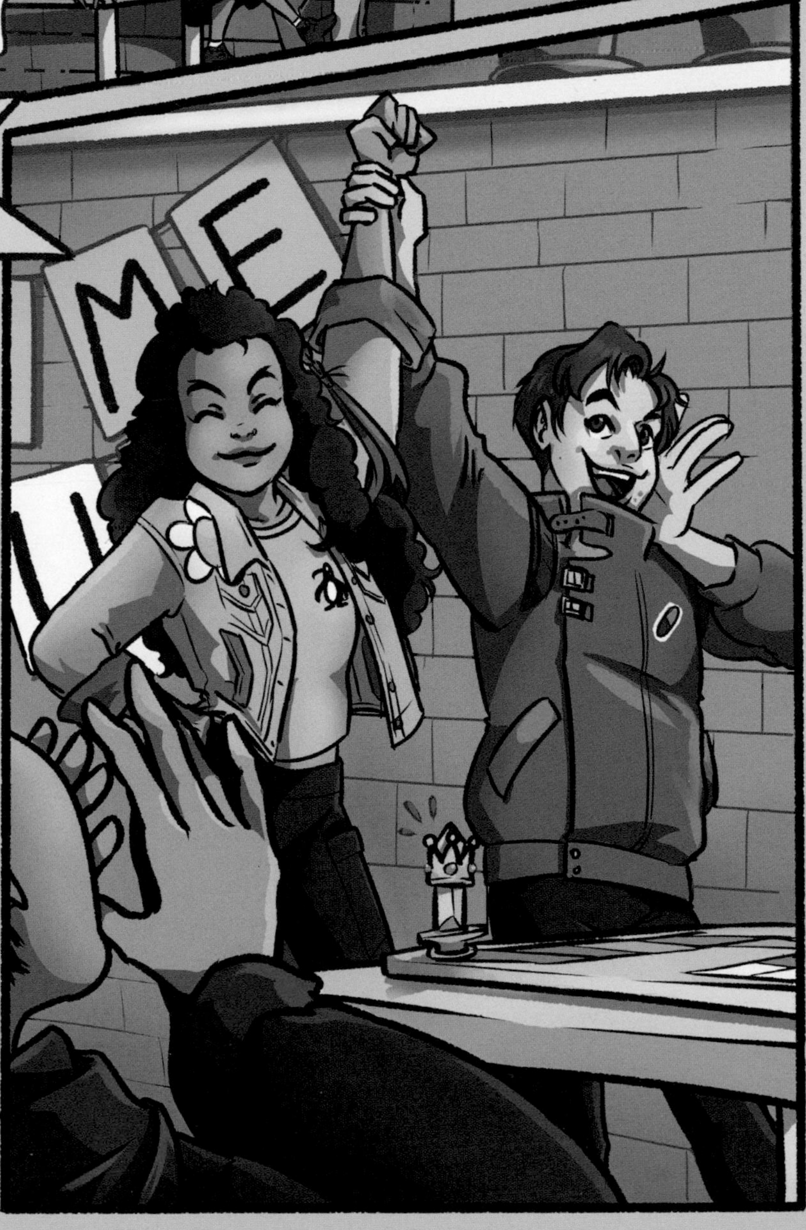
ME

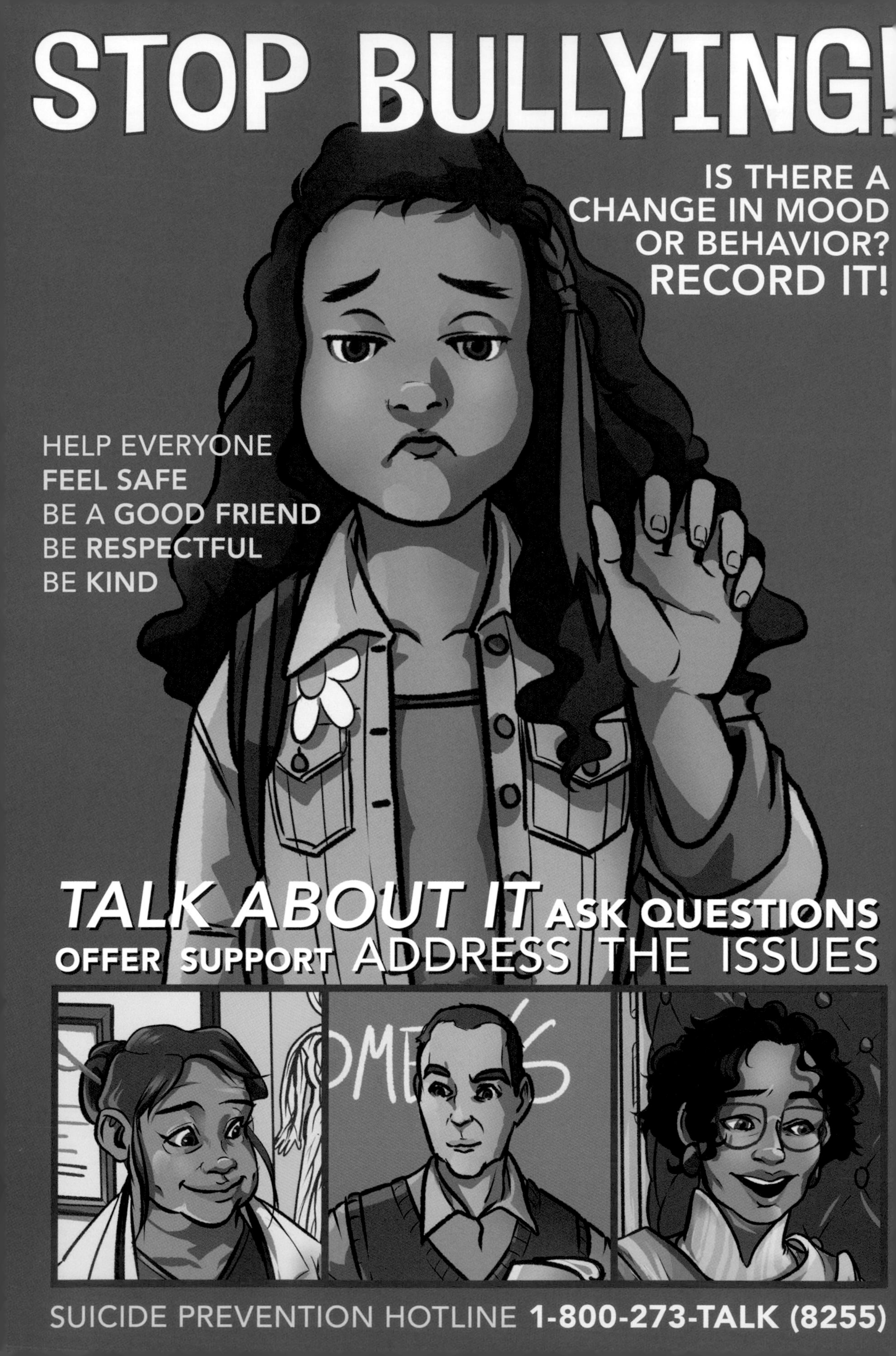

STOP BULLYING!
IS THERE A CHANGE IN MOOD OR BEHAVIOR? RECORD IT!
HELP EVERYONE FEEL SAFE
BE A GOOD FRIEND
BE RESPECTFUL
BE KIND
TALK ABOUT IT ASK QUESTIONS
OFFER SUPPORT ADDRESS THE ISSUES
SUICIDE PREVENTION HOTLINE 1-800-273-TALK (8255)

# ▶▶▶▶▶ BE SWEET AT ◀◀◀◀◀ MEMORIAL MIDDLE SCHOOL

**LILLY:** I'm here on the scene with Mrs. Clark, who's here to tell us about the Be Sweet program she's starting here at Memorial Middle School. This program will reward kids' good behavior toward their classmates. Mrs. Clark's challenge? Be Sweet!

**MRS. CLARK:** Hi Lilly! I'm glad to be here. As you know, bullying has been a recent hot topic here at school. Bullying can have a negative effect on how kids feel about themselves, whether it's in the classroom, at home, or on the playing field. Sometimes bullying can be unintentional, like joking about another student's appearance or style.

**LILLY:** And sometimes it can be intentional!

**MRS. CLARK:** Yes, sometimes it can.

**LILLY:** Why is it so important to talk about bullying, especially now?

**MRS. CLARK:** It's definitely important to talk about bullying when it happens. Anyone can be a bully. And anyone can be bullied—including the bullies! Being picked on can make kids feel helpless and alone.

**LILLY:** But choosing to be kind can help too, right?

**MRS. CLARK:** In my experience, kids do try to be kind. Nobody is telling them to be mean to other kids, right? But people also like to feel helpful. I think that encouraging and rewarding good behavior is a positive thing to practice every day. Thinking about the way you treat others is a great first step to relating to another person.

**LILLY:** Do you have any examples of what kids can do to Be Sweet?

**MRS. CLARK:** Make an effort to know people! Say hi. Ask how someone's day is going. Sit with the kid who's by themselves at lunch, or be partners with someone who doesn't always have one. Offer help to someone who looks like they're struggling. Taking a moment to see when someone is feeling hurt or sad, and then stopping to help them, can go a million miles.

**LILLY:** And sometimes the weird kids can be the most fun!

**MRS. CLARK:** That's right! So get out there and be kind. If a teacher sees you stepping up, you might just earn a sweet reward!

**LILLY:** I think I know exactly what I'm going to do for my first nice thing. Thanks, Mrs. C!

# GLOSSARY

**ANIME** – cartoon movies made in Japan, often using characters and plots taken from written manga

**ANONYMOUS** – written, done, or given by a person whose name is not known or made public

**COSPLAY** – creating or wearing a comic book character costume at a comic book convention

**FOUNDER** – someone who sets up or starts something

**MANIPULATE** – to change something in a clever way to influence people to do or think how you want

**SUFFRAGE** – the right to vote

**TAUNT** – to use words to try to make someone angry

**ZERO-TOLERANCE** – a refusal to accept certain behaviors, such as bullying, without exception

# WHAT DO YOU THINK?

1. Cassie knows what Sami and Tania are doing to Lilly is wrong, but she doesn't stand up to them. Have you ever been in this situation? What did you do?

2. Rewrite part of the the story from Franny's point of view. What part would you focus on?

3. What is your school's policy on bullying? Do you think it's working? How would you change it?

4. Why do you think it took Lilly so long to talk to someone about being bullied?

## CHALLENGE!

Talk to someone you don't know well. Ask them about their interests! Maybe you'll have something in common. Or maybe you'll find a new hobby or interest.

## LOUISE SIMONSON

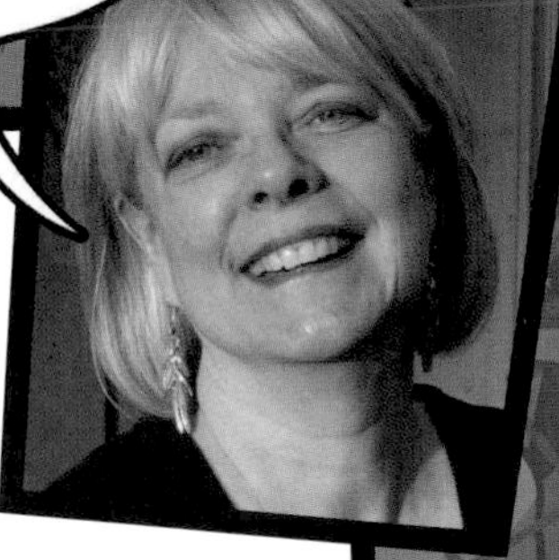

Louise Simonson writes comics and books about monsters, science fiction, and superhero and fantasy characters, including several best-selling X-Men titles, Web of Spider-Man, and Superman: Man of Steel. But her favorite stories star young heroes, like the kids in the award-winning superhero comic Power Pack. She is married to graphic novel artist and writer Walter Simonson and lives in the suburbs of New York City.

## SUMIN CHO

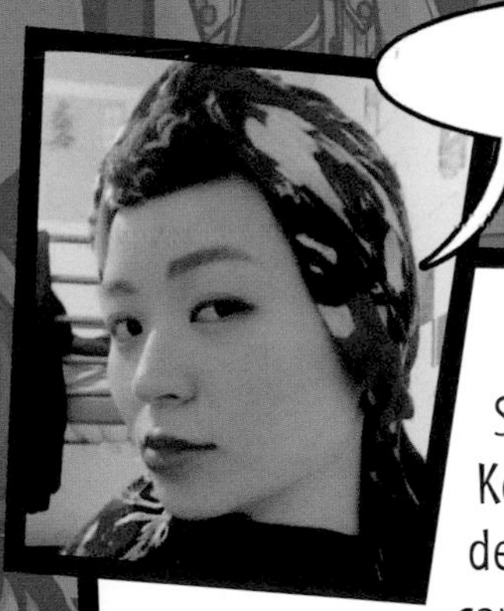

Sumin Cho has spent her childhood in South Korea and New Zealand. She earned her bachelor's degree from Sangmyung University and BFA in cartooning from the School of Visual Arts in New York. She currently lives with two fellow cartoonists along with a dog and cat duo named Puff and Melon.

# WANT MORE DRAMA?

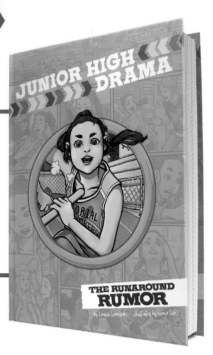

Allie's world is turned upside down when she's diagnosed with diabetes. Her overprotective parents are driving her crazy, and she's desperate to keep her condition a secret from her friends. But her secretive ways are awfully suspicious and soon the rumors are flying. Is Allie's reputation ruined for good?

JUNIOR HIGH DRAMA
THE RUNAROUND RUMOR

JUNIOR HIGH DRAMA
THE SCHOOL MUSICAL MELTDOWN

When Kamilla looks in the mirror, she hates what she sees. Despite being a healthy weight, she feels big and awkward and desperate to hide. But Kamilla is an amazing singer, and she's the perfect choice for a leading role in the school musical. Can Kamilla overcome her fears, or will she be stuck waiting in the wings forever?

The eighth graders at Memorial Middle School are obsessing about their first boy-girl party. Lucia is sick of hearing about what to wear and who's going together. If her best friend hadn't insisted, she wouldn't even go to the dumb party. But after she gets to know Adesh, Lucia starts thinking the party might not be too bad ... until she realizes he's interested in another girl.

JUNIOR HIGH DRAMA
THE FIRST-DATE DILEMMA